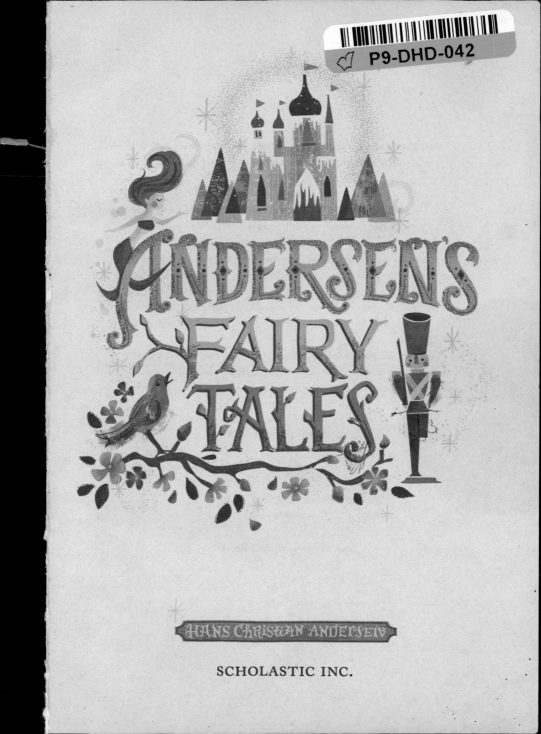

ANDERSEN'S FAIRY TALES

HANS CHRISTIAN ANDERSEN

SCHOLASTIC INC.

CONTENTS

The Emperor's New Suit

Many, many years ago there lived an emperor who thought so much of new clothes that he spent all his money in order to obtain them; his only ambition was to be always well dressed. He did not care for his soldiers, and the theater did amuse him; the only thing, in fact, he thought anything of was to drive around and show a new suit of clothes. He had a coat for every hour of the day; and as one would say of a king, "He is in his cabinet," so one could say of him, "The emperor is in his dressing room."

The great city where he resided was very joyful; every day many strangers from all parts of the globe arrived. One day two swindlers came to this city; they made people believe that they were weavers, and declared they could manufacture the finest cloth to be imagined. Their colors and patterns, they said, were not only exceptionally beautiful, but the clothes made of their material possessed the wonderful quality of being invisible to any man who was unfit for his office or unpardonably stupid.

That must be wonderful cloth, thought the emperor. *If I were to be dressed in a suit made of this cloth I should be able to find out which men in my empire were unfit for their places, and I could distinguish the clever from the stupid. I must have this cloth woven for me without delay.* And he gave a large sum of money to the swindlers, in advance, that they should set to work without any loss of time. They set up two looms, and pretended to be very hard at work, but they did nothing whatever on the looms. They asked for the finest silk and the most precious gold cloth; all they got they did away with, and worked at the empty looms till late at night.

I should very much like to know how they are getting on with the cloth, thought the emperor. But he felt rather uneasy when he remembered that he who was not fit for his office could not see it. Personally, he was of the opinion that he had nothing to fear, yet he thought it advisable to send somebody else first to see how matters stood. Everybody in the town knew what remarkable qualities the cloth possessed, and all were anxious to see how bad or stupid their neighbors were.

I shall send my honest old minister to the weavers, thought the emperor. *He can judge best how the stuff looks, for he is intelligent, and nobody understands his office better than he.*

The good old minister went into the room where the swindlers sat before the empty looms. *Heaven preserve us!* he thought, and opened his eyes wide. *I cannot see anything at all*, but he did not say so. Both swindlers requested him to come near, and asked him if he did not admire the exquisite pattern and the beautiful colors, pointing to the empty looms. The poor old minister tried his very best, but he could see nothing, for there was nothing to be seen. *Oh dear*, he thought, *can I be so stupid? I should never have thought so, and nobody must know it! Is it possible that I am not fit for my office? No, no, I cannot say that I was unable to see the cloth.*

"Now, have you got nothing to say?" said one of the swindlers, while he pretended to be busily weaving.

"Oh, it is very pretty, exceedingly beautiful," replied the old minister, looking through his glasses. "What a beautiful pattern. What brilliant colors! I shall tell the emperor that I like the cloth very much."

"We are pleased to hear that," said the two weavers, and they described to him the colors and explained the curious pattern. The old minister listened attentively, that he might relate to the emperor what they said; and so he did.

Now the swindlers asked for more money, silk, and gold cloth, which they required for weaving. They kept everything for themselves, and not a thread came near the loom, but they continued to work at the empty looms.

Soon afterward the emperor sent another honest courtier to the weavers to see how they were getting on, and if the cloth was nearly finished. Like the old minister, he looked and looked but could see nothing, as there was nothing to be seen.

"Is it not a beautiful piece of cloth?" asked the two swindlers, showing and explaining the magnificent pattern, which, however, did not exist.

"I am not stupid," said the man. "It is therefore my good appointment for which I am not fit. It is very strange, but I must not let anyone know it"; and he praised the cloth, which he did not see, and expressed his joy at the beautiful colors and the fine pattern. "It is very excellent," he said to the emperor.

Everybody in the whole town talked about the precious cloth. At last the emperor wished to see it himself, while it was still on the loom. With a number of courtiers, including the two who had already been there, he went to the two clever swindlers, who now worked as hard as they could, but without using any thread.

"Is it not magnificent?" said the two old statesmen who had been there before. "Your Majesty must admire the colors and the pattern." And then they pointed to the empty looms, for they imagined the others could see the cloth.

What is this? thought the emperor, *I do not see anything at all. That is terrible! Am I stupid? Am I unfit to be emperor? That would indeed be the most dreadful thing that could happen to me.*

"Really," he said, turning to the weavers, "your cloth has our most gracious approval"; and nodding contentedly he looked at the empty loom, for he did not like to say that he saw nothing. All his attendants, who were with him, looked and looked, and although they could not see anything more than the others, they said, like the emperor, "It is very beautiful." And all advised him to wear the new magnificent clothes at a great procession that was soon to take place. "It is magnificent, beautiful, excellent," one heard them say; everybody seemed to be delighted, and the emperor appointed the two swindlers imperial court weavers.

The whole night previous to the day on which the procession was to take place, the swindlers pretended to work, and burned more than sixteen candles. People should see that they were busy to finish the emperor's new suit. They pretended to take the cloth from the loom, and worked about in the air with big scissors, and sewed with needles without thread, and said at last: "The emperor's new suit is ready now."

The emperor and all his barons then came to the hall; the swindlers held their arms up as if they held something in their hands and said: "These are the trousers!"; "This is the coat!"; "Here is the cloak!"; and so on. "They are all as light as a cobweb, and one must feel as if one had nothing at all upon the body; but that is just the beauty of them."

"Indeed!" said all the courtiers; but they could not see anything, for there was nothing to be seen.

"Does it please Your Majesty now to graciously undress," said the swindlers, "so we may assist Your Majesty in putting on the new suit before the large looking glass?"

The emperor undressed, and the swindlers pretended to put the new suit upon him, one piece after another; and the emperor looked at himself in the glass from every side.

"How well they look! How well they fit!" said all. "What a beautiful pattern! What fine colors! That is a magnificent suit of clothes!"

The master of the ceremonies announced that the bearers of the canopy, which was to be carried in the procession, were ready.

"I am ready," said the emperor. "Does not my suit fit me marvelously?" Then he turned once more to the looking glass, that people should think he admired his garments.

The chamberlains, who were to carry the train, stretched their hands to the ground as if they lifted up a train, and pretended to hold something in their hands; they did not like people to know that they could not see anything.

The emperor marched in the procession under the beautiful canopy, and all who saw him in the street and out of the windows exclaimed: "Indeed, the emperor's new suit is incomparable! What a long train he has! How well it fits him!" Nobody wished to let others know they saw nothing, for then they would have been unfit for their office or too stupid. Never were emperor's clothes more admired.

"But he has nothing on at all," said a little child at last. "Good heavens! Listen to the voice of an innocent child," said the father, and one whispered to the other what the child had said. "But he has nothing on at all," cried at last the whole people. That made a deep impression upon the emperor, for it seemed to him that they were right; but he thought to himself, *Now I must bear up to the end*. And the chamberlains walked with still greater dignity, as if they carried the train that did not exist.

The Princess and the Pea

Once upon a time there was a prince who wanted to marry a princess, but she would have to be a real princess. He traveled all over the world to find one, but nowhere could he get what he wanted. There were princesses enough, but it was difficult to find out whether they were real ones. There was always something about them that was not as it should be. So he came home again and was sad, for he would have liked very much to have a real princess.

One evening a terrible storm came on; there was thunder and lightning, and the rain poured down in torrents. Suddenly a knocking was heard at the city gate, and the old king went to open it.

It was a princess standing out there in front of the gate. But good gracious! What a sight the rain and the wind had made her look. The water ran down from her hair and clothes; it ran down into the toes of her shoes and out again at the heels. And yet she said that she was a real princess.

Well, we'll soon find that out, thought the old queen. But she said nothing, went into the bedroom, took all the bedding off the bedstead, and laid a pea on the bottom; then she took twenty mattresses and laid them on the pea, and then twenty eiderdown beds on top of the mattresses.

On this the princess had to lie all night. In the morning she was asked how she had slept.

"Oh, very badly!" said she. "I have scarcely closed my eyes all night. Heaven only knows what was in the bed, but I was lying on something hard, so that I am black and blue all over my body. It's horrible!"

Now they knew that she was a real princess because she had felt the pea right through the twenty mattresses and the twenty eiderdown beds.

Nobody but a real princess could be as sensitive as that.

So the prince took her for his wife, for now he knew that he had a real princess, and the pea was put in the museum, where it may still be seen, if no one has stolen it.

There, that is a true story.

The Steadfast Tin Soldier

There were once five-and-twenty tin soldiers, who were all brothers, for they had been made out of the same old tin spoon. They shouldered arms and looked straight before them, and wore a splendid uniform, red and blue. The first thing in the world they ever heard were the words "Tin soldiers!" uttered by a little boy who clapped his hands with delight when the lid of the box in which they lay was taken off. They were given him for a birthday present, and he stood at the table to set them up. The soldiers were all exactly alike, except one, who had only one leg; he had been left to the last, and then there was not enough of the melted tin to finish him, so they made him to stand firmly on one leg, and this caused him to be very remarkable.

The table on which the tin soldiers stood was covered with other playthings, but the most attractive to the eye was a pretty little paper castle. Through the small windows the rooms could be seen. In front of the castle a number of little trees surrounded a piece of looking glass, which was intended to represent a transparent lake. Swans, made of wax, swam on the lake, and were reflected in it. All this was very pretty, but the prettiest of all was a tiny little lady, who stood at the open door of the castle; she, also, was made of paper, and she wore a dress of clear muslin, with a narrow blue ribbon over her shoulders just like a scarf. In front of these was fixed a glittering tinsel rose, as large as her whole face. The little lady was a dancer, and she stretched out both her arms, and raised one of her legs so high that the tin soldier could not see it at all, and he thought that she, like himself, had only one leg. *That is the wife for me*, he thought, *but she is too grand, and lives in a castle, while I have only a box to live in, five-and-twenty of us altogether, that is no place for her. Still I must try to make her acquaintance.* Then he laid himself at full length on the table behind a snuff box that stood upon it, so that he could peep at the little delicate lady, who continued to stand on one leg without losing her balance. When evening came, the other tin soldiers were all placed in the box, and the people of the house went to bed. Then the playthings began to have their own games together, to pay visits, to have play fights, and to give balls. The tin soldiers rattled in their box; they wanted to get out and join the amusements, but they could not open the lid. The nutcrackers played at leapfrog, and the pencil jumped about the table. There was such a noise that the canary woke up and began to talk, and in poetry, too. Only the tin soldier and the dancer remained in their places. She stood on tiptoe, with her legs stretched out, as firmly as he did on his one leg. He never took his eyes from her for even a moment.

The clock struck twelve, and, with a bounce, up sprang the lid of the snuff box; but, instead of snuff, there jumped up a little black goblin; for the snuff box was a toy puzzle.

"Tin soldier," said the goblin, "don't wish for what does not belong to you."

But the tin soldier pretended not to hear.

"Very well; wait till tomorrow, then," said the goblin.

When the children came in the next morning, they placed the tin soldier in the window. Now, whether it was the goblin who did it, or the draft, is not known, but the window flew open, and out fell the tin soldier, heel overhead, from the third story, into the street beneath. It was a terrible fall; for he came head downward, his helmet and his bayonet stuck in between the flagstones, and his one leg up in the air. The servant maid and the little boy went downstairs directly to look for him; but he was nowhere to be seen, although once they nearly trod upon him. If he had called out, "Here I am," it would have been all right, but he was too proud to cry out for help while he wore a uniform.

Presently it began to rain, and the drops fell faster and faster, till there was a heavy shower. When it was over, two boys happened to pass by, and one of them said, "Look, there is a tin soldier. He ought to have a boat to sail in."

So they made a boat out of a newspaper, and placed the tin soldier in it, and sent him sailing down the gutter, while the two boys ran by the side of it, and clapped their hands. Good gracious, what large waves arose in that gutter! And how fast the stream rolled on! For the rain had been very heavy. The paper boat rocked up and down, and turned itself around sometimes so quickly that the tin soldier trembled, yet he remained firm; his countenance did not change; he looked straight before him, and shouldered his musket. Suddenly the boat shot under a bridge, which formed a part of a drain, and then it was as dark as the tin soldier's box.

Where am I going now? thought he. *This is the black goblin's fault, I am sure. Ah, well, if the little lady were only here with me in the boat, I should not care for any darkness.*

Suddenly there appeared a great water rat, who lived in the drain.

"Have you a passport?" asked the rat. "Give it to me at once." But the tin soldier remained silent and held his musket tighter than ever. The boat sailed on and the rat followed it. How he did gnash his teeth and cry out to the bits of wood and straw, "Stop him, stop him; he has not paid toll, and has not shown his pass." But the stream rushed on stronger and stronger. The tin soldier could already see daylight shining where the arch ended. Then he heard a roaring sound quite terrible enough to frighten the bravest man. At the end of the tunnel the drain fell into a large canal over a steep place, which made it as dangerous for him as a waterfall would be to us. He was too close to it to stop, so the boat rushed on, and the poor tin soldier could only hold himself as stiffly as possible, without moving an eyelid, to show that he was not afraid. The boat whirled around three or four times, and then filled with water to the very edge; nothing could save it from sinking. He now stood up to his neck in water, while deeper and deeper sank the boat, and the paper became soft and loose with the wet, till at last the water closed over the soldier's head. He thought of the elegant little dancer whom he should never see again, and the words of the song sounded in his ears:

"Farewell, warrior! Ever brave,

Drifting onward to thy grave."

Then the paper boat fell to pieces, and the soldier sank into the water and immediately afterward was swallowed up by a great fish. Oh, how dark it was inside the fish! A great deal darker than in the tunnel, and narrower, too, but the tin soldier continued firm, and lay at full length shouldering his musket. The fish swam to and fro, making the most wonderful movements, but at last he became quite still. After a while, a flash of lightning seemed to pass through him, and then the daylight approached, and a voice cried out, "I declare, here is the tin soldier." The fish had been caught, taken to the market, and sold to the cook, who took him into the kitchen and cut him open with a large knife. She picked up the soldier and held him by the waist between her finger and thumb, and carried him into the room. They were all anxious to see this wonderful soldier who had traveled about inside a fish, but he was not at all proud. They placed him on the table, and—how many curious things do happen in the world!—there he was in the very same room with the window from which he had fallen, there were the same children, the same playthings, standing on the table, and the pretty castle with the elegant little dancer at the door; she still balanced herself on one leg, and held up the other, so she was as firm as himself. It touched the tin soldier so much to see her that he almost wept tin tears, but he kept them back. He only looked at her and they both remained silent. Presently one of the little boys took up the tin soldier, and threw him into the stove. He had no reason for doing so; therefore it must have been the fault of the black goblin who lived in the snuff box. The flames lighted up the tin soldier as he stood; the heat was very terrible, but whether it proceeded from the real fire or from the fire of love he could not tell. Then he could see that the bright colors were faded from his uniform, but whether they had been washed off during his journey or from the effects of his sorrow, no one could say. He looked at the little lady, and she looked at him. He felt himself melting away, but he still remained firm with his gun on his shoulder. Suddenly the door of the room flew open and the draft of air caught up the little dancer; she fluttered right into the stove by the side of the tin soldier, and was instantly in flames and was gone. The tin soldier melted down into a lump, and the next morning, when the maid servant took the ashes out of the stove, she found him in the shape of a little tin heart. But of the little dancer nothing remained but the tinsel rose, which was burned black as a cinder.

Thumbelina

There was once a woman who wished very much to have a little child, but she could not obtain her wish. At last she went to a fairy and said, "I should so very much like to have a little child; can you tell me where I can find one?"

"Oh, that can be easily managed," said the fairy. "Here is a barleycorn of a different kind from those that grow in the farmer's fields and that the chickens eat; put it into a flowerpot, and see what will happen."

"Thank you," said the woman, and she gave the fairy twelve shillings, which was the price of the barleycorn. Then she went home and planted it, and immediately there grew up a large handsome flower, something like a tulip in appearance, but with its leaves tightly closed as if it were still a bud. "It is a beautiful flower," said the woman, and she kissed the red- and golden-colored leaves, and while she did so the flower opened, and she could see that it was a real tulip. Within the flower, upon the green velvet stamens, sat a very delicate and graceful little maiden. She was scarcely half as long as a thumb, and gave her the name of Thumbelina, or Tiny, because she was so small. A walnut shell, elegantly polished, served her for a cradle; her bed was formed of blue violet leaves, with a rose leaf for a bedspread. Here she slept at night, but during the day she amused herself on a table, where the woman had placed a plateful of water. Around this plate were wreaths of flowers with their stems in the water, and upon it floated a large tulip leaf, which served Tiny for a boat. Here the little maiden sat and rowed herself from side to side, with two oars made of white horsehair. It really was a very pretty sight. Tiny could also sing so softly and sweetly that nothing like her singing had ever before been heard. One night, while she lay in her pretty bed, a large, ugly wet toad crept through a broken pane of glass in the window, and leaped right upon the table where Tiny lay sleeping under her rose-leaf quilt.

"What a pretty little wife this would make for my son," said the toad, and she took up the walnut shell in which little Tiny lay asleep, and jumped through the window with it into the garden.

In the swampy margin of a broad stream in the garden lived the toad with her son. He was uglier even than his mother, and when he saw the pretty little maiden in her elegant bed, he could only cry, "Croak, croak, croak."

"Don't speak so loud, or she will wake," said the toad, "and then she might run away, for she is as light as swan's down. We will place her on one of the water lily leaves out in the stream; it will be like an island to her, she is so light and small, and then she cannot escape; and, while she is away, we will make haste and prepare the stateroom under the marsh, in which you are to live when you are married."

Far out in the stream grew a number of water lilies, with broad green leaves, which seemed to float on the top of the water. The largest of these leaves appeared farther off than the rest, and the old toad swam out to it with the walnut shell, in which little Tiny lay still asleep. The tiny little creature woke very early in the morning and began to cry bitterly when she found where she was, for she could see nothing but water on every side of the large green leaf, and no way of reaching the land. Meanwhile the old toad was very busy under the marsh, decking her room with rushes and wild yellow flowers, to make it look pretty for her new daughter-in-law. Then she swam out with her ugly son to the leaf on which she had placed poor little Tiny. She wanted to fetch the pretty bed, that she might put it in the bridal chamber to be ready for her. The old toad bowed low to her in the water and said,

"Here is my son. He will be your husband, and you will live happily in the marsh by the stream."

"Croak, croak, croak," was all her son could say for himself; so the toad took up the elegant little bed, and swam away with it, leaving Tiny all alone on the green leaf, where she sat and wept. She could not bear to think of living with the old toad and having her ugly son for a husband. The little fishes, who swam about in the water beneath, had seen the toad, and heard what she said, so they lifted their heads above the water to look at the little maiden. As soon as they caught sight of her, they saw she was very pretty, and it made them very sorry to think that she must go and live with the ugly toads. "No, it must never be!" So they assembled together in the water, around the green stalk that held the leaf on which the little maiden stood, and gnawed it away at the root with their teeth. Then the leaf floated down the stream, carrying Tiny far away out of reach of land.

Tiny sailed past many towns, and the little birds in the bushes saw her, and sang, "What a lovely little creature"; so the leaf swam away with her farther and farther, till it brought her to other lands. A graceful little white butterfly constantly fluttered around her, and at last alighted on the leaf. Tiny pleased him, and she was glad of it, for now the toad could not possibly reach her, and the country through which she sailed was beautiful, and the sun shone upon the water till it glittered like liquid gold. She took off her girdle and tied one end of it around the butterfly, and the other end of the ribbon she fastened to the leaf, which now glided on much faster than ever, taking little Tiny with it as she stood. Presently a large beetle flew by. The moment he caught sight of her, he seized her around her delicate waist with his claws, and flew with her into a tree. The green leaf floated away on the brook, and the butterfly flew with it, for he was fastened to it and could not get away.

Oh, how frightened little Tiny felt when the beetle flew with her to the tree! But especially was she sorry for the beautiful white butterfly that she had fastened to the leaf, for if he could not free himself he would die of hunger. But the insect did not trouble himself at all about the matter. He seated himself by her side on a large green leaf, gave her some honey from the flowers to eat, and told her she was very pretty, though not in the least like a beetle. After a time, all the beetles turned up their feelers, and said, "She has only two legs! How ugly that looks."

"She has no feelers," said another.

"Her waist is quite slim. Pooh! She is like a human being."

"Oh! She is ugly," said all the lady beetles, although Tiny was very pretty. Then the insect who had run away with her believed all the others when they said she was ugly, and would have nothing more to say to her, and told her she might go where she liked. Then he flew down with her from the tree and placed her on a daisy, and she wept at the thought that she was so ugly that even the beetles would have nothing to say to her. And all the while she was really the loveliest creature that one could imagine and as tender and delicate as a beautiful rose leaf. During the whole summer, poor little Tiny lived quite alone in the wide forest. She wove herself a bed with blades of grass, and hung it up under a broad leaf, to protect herself from the rain. She sucked the honey from the flowers for food, and drank the dew from their leaves every morning. So passed away the summer and the autumn, and then came the winter—the long, cold winter. All the birds who had sung to her so sweetly were flown away, and the trees and the flowers had withered. The large clover leaf under the shelter of which she had lived was now rolled together and shriveled up; nothing remained but a yellow withered stalk. She felt dreadfully cold, for her clothes were torn, and she was herself so frail and delicate that poor little Tiny was nearly frozen to death. It began to snow, too; and the snowflakes, as they fell upon her, were like a whole shovelful falling upon one of us, for we are tall, but she was only an inch high. Then she wrapped herself up in a dry leaf, but it cracked in the middle and could not keep her warm, and she shivered with cold. Near the wood in which she had been living lay a cornfield, but the corn had been cut a long time; nothing remained but the bare dry stubble standing up out of the frozen ground. It was to her like struggling through a large wood. Oh! How she shivered with the cold. She came at last to the door of a field mouse, who had a little den under the corn stubble. There dwelt the field mouse in warmth and comfort, with a whole roomful of corn, a kitchen, and a beautiful dining room. Poor little Tiny stood before the door just like a little beggar girl, and begged for a small piece of barleycorn, for she had been without a morsel to eat for two days.

"You poor little creature," said the field mouse, who was really a good old field mouse. "Come into my warm room and dine with me." She was very pleased with Tiny, so she said, "You are quite welcome to stay with me all the winter, if you like; but you must keep my rooms clean and neat, and tell me stories, for I shall like to hear them very much." And Tiny did all the field mouse asked of her, and found herself very comfortable.

"We shall have a visitor soon," said the field mouse one day. "My neighbor pays me a visit once a week. He is better off than I am; he has large rooms and wears a beautiful black velvet coat. If you could only have him for a husband, you would be well provided for, indeed. But he is blind, so you must tell him some of your prettiest stories."

But Tiny did not feel at all interested about this neighbor, for he was a mole. However, he came and paid his visit dressed in his black velvet coat.

"He is very rich and learned, and his house is twenty times larger than mine," said the field mouse.

He was rich and learned, no doubt, but he always spoke slightingly of the sun and the pretty flowers, because he had never seen them. Tiny was obliged to sing to him, "Ladybug, Ladybug, Fly Away Home," and many other pretty songs. And the mole fell in love with her because she had such a sweet voice; but he said nothing yet, for he was very cautious. A short time before, the mole had dug a long passage under the earth, which led from the dwelling of the field mouse to his own, and here she had permission to walk with Tiny whenever she liked. But he warned them not to be alarmed at the sight of a dead bird, which lay in the passage. It was a perfect bird, with a beak and feathers, and could not have been dead long, and was lying just where the mole had made his passage. The mole took a piece of phosphorescent wood in his mouth, and it glittered like fire in the dark; then he went before them to light them through the long, dark passage. When they came to the spot where lay the dead bird, the mole pushed his broad nose through the ceiling. The earth gave way so that there was a large hole, and the daylight shone into the passage. In the middle of the floor lay a dead swallow, his beautiful wings pulled close to his sides, his feet and his head drawn up under his feathers; the poor bird had evidently died of the cold. It made little Tiny very sad to see it, she did so love the little birds; all the summer they had sung and twittered for her so beautifully. But the mole pushed it aside with his crooked legs, and said, "He will sing no more now. How miserable it must be to be born a little bird! I am thankful that none of my children will ever be birds, for they can do nothing but cry, 'Tweet, tweet,' and always die of hunger in the winter."

"Yes, you may well say that as a clever man!" exclaimed the field mouse. "What is the use of his twittering, for when winter comes he must either starve or be frozen to death. Still birds are very high bred."

Tiny said nothing; but when the two others had turned their backs on the bird, she stooped down and stroked aside the soft feathers, which covered the head, and kissed the closed eyelids. "Perhaps this was the one who sang to me so sweetly in the summer," she said. "And how much pleasure it gave me, you dear, pretty bird."

The mole now stopped up the hole through which the daylight shone, and then accompanied the lady home. But during the night Tiny could not sleep, so she got out of bed and wove a large, beautiful carpet of hay; then she carried it to the dead bird, and spread it over him with some down from the flowers, which she had found in the field mouse's room. It was as soft as wool, and she spread some of it on each side of the bird, so that he might lie warmly in the cold earth. "Farewell, you pretty little bird," said she. "Farewell; thank you for your delightful singing during the summer, when all the trees were green and the warm sun shone upon us." Then she laid her head on the bird's breast, but she was alarmed immediately, for it seemed as if something inside the bird went *thump, thump*. It was the bird's heart; he was not really dead, only benumbed with the cold, and the warmth had restored him to life. In autumn, all the swallows fly away into warm countries, but if one happens to linger the cold seizes it, it becomes frozen, and falls down as if dead; it remains where it fell, and the cold snow covers it. Tiny trembled very much; she was quite frightened, for the bird was large, a great deal larger than herself— she was only an inch high. But she took courage, laid the wool more thickly over the poor swallow, and then took a leaf that she had used for her own counterpane, and laid it over the head of the poor bird. The next morning she again stole out to see him. He was alive but very weak; he could only open his eyes for a moment to look at Tiny, who stood by holding a piece of decayed wood in her hand, for she had no other lantern. "Thank you, pretty little maiden," said the sick swallow. "I have been so nicely warmed that I shall soon regain my strength and be able to fly about again in the warm sunshine."

"Oh," said she, "it is cold out of doors now; it snows and freezes. Stay in your warm bed; I will take care of you."

Then she brought the swallow some water in a flower leaf, and after he had drank, he told her that he had wounded one of his wings in a thornbush, and could not fly as fast as the others, who were soon far away on their journey to warm countries. Then at last he had fallen to the earth and could remember no more, nor how he came to be where she had found him. The whole winter the swallow remained underground, and Tiny nursed him with care and love. Neither the mole nor the field mouse knew anything about it, for they did not like swallows. Very soon the spring time came, and the sun warmed the earth. Then the swallow bade farewell to Tiny, and she opened the hole in the ceiling, which the mole had made. The sun shone in upon them so beautifully that the swallow asked her if she would go with him; she could sit on his back, he said, and he would fly away with her into the green woods. But Tiny knew it would make the field mouse very grieved if she left her in that manner, so she said, "No, I cannot."

"Farewell, then. Farewell, you good, pretty little maiden," said the swallow; and he flew out into the sunshine.

Tiny looked after him, and the tears rose in her eyes. She was very fond of the poor swallow.

"Tweet, tweet," sang the bird, as he flew out into the green woods, and Tiny felt very sad. She was not allowed to go out into the warm sunshine. The corn, which had been sown in the field over the house of the field mouse, had grown up high into the air, and formed a thick wood to Tiny, who was only an inch in height.

"You are going to be married, Tiny," said the field mouse. "My neighbor has asked for you. What good fortune for a poor child like you. Now we will prepare your wedding clothes. They must be both woolen and linen. Nothing must be wanting when you are the mole's wife."

Tiny had to turn the spindle, and the field mouse hired four spiders, who were to weave day and night. Every evening the mole visited her, and was continually speaking of the time when the summer would be over. Then he would keep his wedding day with Tiny; but now the heat of the sun was so great that it burned the earth, and made it quite hard, like a stone. As soon as the summer was over, the wedding should take place. But Tiny was not at all pleased, for she did not like the tiresome mole. Every morning when the sun rose and every evening when it went down, she would creep out the door, and as the wind blew aside the ears of corn so that she could see the blue sky, she thought how beautiful and bright it seemed out there and wished so much to see her dear swallow again. But he never returned, for by this time he had flown far away into the lovely green forest.

When autumn arrived, Tiny had her outfit quite ready, and the field mouse said to her, "In four weeks the wedding must take place."

Then Tiny wept and said she would not marry the disagreeable mole.

"Nonsense," replied the field mouse. "Now don't be obstinate, or I shall bite you with my white teeth. He is a very handsome mole; the queen herself does not wear more beautiful velvets and furs. His kitchen and cellars are quite full. You ought to be very thankful for such good fortune."

So the wedding day was fixed, on which the mole was to fetch Tiny away to live with him deep under the earth, and never again to see the warm sun because he did not like it. The poor child was very unhappy at the thought of saying farewell to the beautiful sun and as the field mouse had given her permission to stand at the door, she went to look at it once more.

"Farewell, bright sun," she cried, stretching out her arm toward it, and then she walked a short distance from the house; for the corn had been cut, and only the dry stubble remained in the fields. "Farewell, farewell," she repeated, twining her arm around a little red flower that grew just by her side. "Greet the little swallow for me, if you should see him again."

"Tweet, tweet," sounded over her head suddenly. She looked up, and there was the swallow himself flying close by. As soon as he spied Tiny he was delighted, and then she told him how unwilling she felt to marry the ugly mole and to live always beneath the earth, never to see the bright sun anymore. And as she told him she wept.

"Cold winter is coming," said the swallow, "and I am going to fly away into warmer countries. Will you go with me? You can sit on my back and fasten yourself on with your sash. Then we can fly away from the ugly mole and his gloomy rooms—far away, over the mountains, into warmer countries, where the sun shines more brightly— where it is always summer, and the flowers bloom in greater beauty. Fly now with me, dear little Tiny, you saved my life when I lay frozen in that dark passage."

"Yes, I will go with you," said Tiny, and she seated herself on the bird's back, with her feet on his outstretched wings, and tied her girdle to one of his strongest feathers.

Then the swallow rose in the air and flew over forest and over sea, high above the highest mountains, covered with eternal snow. Tiny would have been frozen in the cold air, but she crept under the bird's warm feathers, keeping her little head uncovered, so that she might admire the beautiful lands over which they passed. At length they reached the warm countries, where the sun shines brightly and the sky seems so much higher above the earth. Here on the hedges and by the wayside, grew purple, green, and white grapes; lemons and oranges hung from trees in the woods; and the air was fragrant with myrtles and orange blossoms. Beautiful children ran along the country lanes, playing with large butterflies, and as the swallow flew farther and farther, every place appeared still more lovely.

At last they came to a blue lake, and by the side of it, shaded by trees of the deepest green, stood a palace of dazzling white marble, built in the olden times. Vines clustered around its lofty pillars, and at the top were many swallows' nests, and one of these was the home of the swallow who carried Tiny.

"This is my house," said the swallow, "but it would not do for you to live here—you would not be comfortable. You must choose for yourself one of those lovely flowers, and I will put you down upon it, and then you shall have everything that you can wish to make you happy."

"That will be delightful," she said and clapped her little hands for joy.

A large marble pillar lay on the ground, which, in falling, had been broken into three pieces. Between these pieces grew the most beautiful large white flowers, so the swallow flew down with Tiny and placed her on one of the broad leaves. But how surprised she was to see in the middle of the flower a tiny little man, as white and transparent as if he had been made of crystal! He had a gold crown on his head and delicate wings at his shoulders and was not much larger than Tiny herself. He was the angel of the flower—for a tiny man and a tiny woman dwell in every flower—and this was the king of them all.

"Oh, how beautiful he is!" whispered Tiny to the swallow.

The little prince was at first quite frightened at the bird, who was like a giant compared to such a delicate little creature as himself, but when he saw Tiny he was delighted and thought her the prettiest little maiden he had ever seen. He took the gold crown from his head and placed it on hers and asked her name and if she would be his wife and queen over all the flowers.

This certainly was a very different sort of husband to the son of a toad or the mole with black velvet and fur, so she said yes to the handsome prince. Then all the flowers opened and out of each came a little lady or a tiny lord, all so pretty it was quite a pleasure to look at them. Each of them brought Tiny a present, but the best gift was a pair of beautiful wings, which had belonged to a large white fly, and they fastened them to Tiny's shoulders so that she might fly from flower to flower. Then there was much rejoicing, and the little swallow who sat above them in his nest, was asked to sing a wedding song, which he did as well as he could; but in his heart he felt sad, for he was very fond of Tiny, and would have liked never to part from her again.

"You must not be called Tiny anymore," said the spirit of the flowers to her. "It is an ugly name, and you are so very pretty. We will call you Maia."

"Farewell, farewell," said the swallow with a heavy heart as he left the warm countries to fly back into Denmark. There he had a nest over the window of a house in which dwelt the writer of fairy tales. The swallow sang, "Tweet, tweet," and from his song came the whole story.

Jack the Dullard

An Old Story Told Anew

Far in the interior of the country lay an old baronial hall, and in it lived an old proprietor who had two sons, which two young men thought themselves too clever by half. They wanted to go out and woo the king's daughter, for the maiden in question had publicly announced that she would choose for her husband that youth who could arrange his words best.

So these two geniuses prepared themselves a full week for the wooing—this was the longest time that could be granted them; but it was enough, for they had had much preparatory information, and everybody knows how useful that is. One of them knew the whole Latin dictionary by heart, and three whole years of the daily paper of the little town into the bargain, and so well, indeed, that he could repeat it all either backward or forward, just as he chose. The other was deeply read in the corporation laws and knew by heart what every corporation ought to know; and, accordingly, he thought he could talk of affairs of state and put his spoke in the wheel in the council. And he knew one thing more: He could embroider suspenders with roses and other flowers, and with arabesques, for he was a tasty, light-fingered fellow.

"I shall win the princess!" so cried both of them. Therefore their old papa gave to each of them a handsome horse. The youth who knew the dictionary and newspaper by heart had a black horse, and he who knew all about the corporation laws received a milk-white steed. Then they rubbed the corners of their mouths with fish oil, so that they might become very smooth and glib. All the servants stood below in the courtyard and looked on while they mounted their horses, and just by chance the third son came up. For the proprietor had really three sons, though nobody counted the third with his brothers, because he was not so learned as they, and indeed he was generally known as "Jack the Dullard."

"Hallo!" said Jack the Dullard. "Where are you going? I declare you have put on your Sunday clothes!"

"We're going to the king's court, as suitors to the king's daughter. Don't you know the announcement that has been made all through the country?" And they told him all about it.

"My word! I'll be in it, too!" cried Jack the Dullard, and his two brothers burst out laughing at him and rode away.

"Father, dear," said Jack, "I must have a horse, too. I do feel so desperately inclined to marry! If she accepts me, she accepts me; and if she won't have me, I'll have her; but she shall be mine!"

"Don't talk nonsense," replied the old gentleman. "You shall have no horse from me. You don't know how to speak—you can't arrange your words. Your brothers are very different fellows from you."

"Well," said Jack the Dullard, "if I can't have a horse, I'll take the billy goat, who belongs to me, and he can carry me very well!"

And so said, so done. He mounted the billy goat, pressed his heels into its sides, and galloped down the high street like a hurricane.

"Hei, houp! That was a ride! Here I come!" shouted Jack the Dullard, and he sang till his voice echoed far and wide.

But his brothers rode slowly on in advance of him. They spoke not a word, for they were thinking about the fine speeches they would have to bring out, and these had to be cleverly prepared beforehand.

"Hallo!" shouted Jack the Dullard. "Here am I! Look what I have found on the high road." And he showed them what it was, and it was a dead crow.

"Dullard!" exclaimed the brothers. "What are you going to do with that?"

"With the crow? Why, I am going to give it to the princess."

"Yes, do so," said they, and they laughed and rode on.

"Hallo, here I am again! Just see what I have found now: You don't find that on the high road every day!"

And the brothers turned around to see what he could have found now.

"Dullard!" they cried. "That is only an old wooden shoe, and the upper part is missing into the bargain. Are you going to give that also to the princess?"

"Most certainly I shall," replied Jack the Dullard, and again the brothers laughed and rode on, and thus they got far in advance of him, but—

"Hallo—hop rara!" and there was Jack the Dullard again. "It is getting better and better," he cried. "Hurrah! It is quite famous."

"Why, what have you found this time?" inquired the brothers.

"Oh," said Jack the Dullard, "I can hardly tell you. How glad the princess will be!"

"Bah!" said the brothers. "That is nothing but clay out of the ditch."

"Yes, certainly it is," said Jack the Dullard, "and clay of the finest sort. See, it is so wet, it runs through one's fingers." And he filled his pocket with the clay.

But his brothers galloped on till the sparks flew, and, consequently, they arrived a full hour earlier at the town gate than could Jack. Now at the gate each suitor was provided with a number, and all were placed in rows immediately on their arrival—six in each row—and so closely packed together that they could not move their arms; and that was a prudent arrangement, for they would certainly have come to blows, had they been able, merely because one of them stood before the other.

All the inhabitants of the country stood in great crowds around the castle, almost under the very windows, to see the princess receive the suitors; and as each stepped into the hall, his power of speech seemed to desert him, like the light of a candle that is blown out. Then the princess would say, "He is of no use! Away with him out of the hall!"

At last the turn came for that brother who knew the dictionary by heart, but he did not know it now. He had absolutely forgotten it altogether, and the boards seemed to re-echo with his footsteps, and the ceiling of the hall was made of looking glass, so that he saw himself standing on his head; and at the window stood three clerks and a head clerk, and every one of them was writing down every single word that was uttered, so that it might be printed in the newspapers, and sold for a penny at the street corners. It was a terrible ordeal, and they had, moreover, made such a fire in the stove that the room seemed quite red hot.

"It is dreadfully hot here!" observed the first brother.

"Yes," replied the princess, "my father is going to roast young pullets today."

"Baa!" There he stood like a baa-lamb. He had not been prepared for a speech of this kind, and had not a word to say, though he intended to say something witty. "Baa!"

"He is of no use!" said the princess. "Away with him!"

And he was obliged to go accordingly. And now the second brother came in.

"It is terribly warm here!" he observed.

"Yes, we're roasting pullets today," replied the princess.

"What—what were you—were you pleased to ob—" stammered he, and all the clerks wrote down, "pleased to ob—"

"He is of no use!" said the princess. "Away with him!"

Now came the turn of Jack the Dullard. He rode into the hall on his goat.

"Well, it's most abominably hot here."

"Yes, because I'm roasting young pullets," replied the princess.

"Ah, that's lucky!" exclaimed Jack the Dullard. "For I suppose you'll let me roast my crow at the same time?"

"With the greatest pleasure," said the princess. "But have you anything you can roast it in? For I have neither pot nor pan."

"Certainly I have!" said Jack. "Here's a cooking utensil with a tin handle."

And he brought out the old wooden shoe, and put the crow into it.

"Well, that is a famous dish!" said the princess. "But what shall we do for sauce?"

"Oh, I have that in my pocket," said Jack. "I have so much of it that I can afford to throw some away," and he poured some of the clay out of his pocket.

"I like that!" said the princess. "You can give an answer and you have something to say for yourself, so you shall be my husband. But are you aware that every word we speak is being taken down and will be published in the paper tomorrow? Look yonder, and you will see in every window three clerks and a head clerk; and the old head clerk is the worst of all, for he can't understand anything."

But she only said this to frighten Jack the Dullard; and the clerks gave a great crow of delight, and each one spurted a blot out of his pen onto the floor.

"Oh, those are the gentlemen, are they?" said Jack. "Then I will give the best I have to the head clerk." And he turned out his pockets and flung the wet clay full in the head clerk's face.

"That was very cleverly done," observed the princess. "I could not have done that, but I shall learn in time."

And accordingly Jack the Dullard was made a king, and received a crown and a wife, and sat upon a throne. And this report we have wet from the press of the head clerk and the corporation of printers—but they are not to be depended upon in the least.

The Little Mermaid

Far out in the ocean, where the water is as blue as the prettiest cornflower and as clear as crystal, it is very, very deep; so deep, indeed, that no cable could fathom it: Many church steeples, piled one upon another, would not reach from the ground beneath to the surface of the water above. There dwell the Sea King and his subjects. We must not imagine that there is nothing at the bottom of the sea but bare yellow sand. No, indeed; the most singular flowers and plants grow there; the leaves and stems of which are so pliant that the slightest agitation of the water causes them to stir as if they had life. Fishes, both large and small, glide between the branches, as birds fly among the trees here upon land. In the deepest spot of all stands the castle of the Sea King. Its walls are built of coral, and the long, gothic windows are of the clearest amber. The roof is formed of shells that open and close as the water flows over them. Their appearance is very beautiful, for in each lies a glittering pearl, which would be fit for the diadem of a queen.

The Sea King had been a widower for many years, and his aged mother kept house for him. She was a very wise woman and exceedingly proud of her high birth; on that account she wore twelve oysters on her tail, while others, also of high rank, were only allowed to wear six. She was, however, deserving of very great praise, especially for her care of the little sea princesses, her granddaughters. They were six beautiful children, but the youngest was the prettiest of them all; her skin was as clear and delicate as a rose leaf, and her eyes as blue as the deepest sea; but, like all the others, she had no feet, and her body ended in a fish's tail. All day long they played in the great halls of the castle or among the living flowers that grew out of the walls. The large amber windows were open, and the fish swam in, just as the swallows fly into our houses when we open the windows, except that the fishes swam up to the princesses, ate out of their hands, and allowed themselves to be stroked. Outside the castle there was a beautiful garden, in which grew bright red and dark blue flowers and blossoms like flames of fire; the fruit glittered like gold, and the leaves and stems waved to and fro continually. The earth itself was the finest sand, but blue as the flame of burning sulfur. Over everything lay a peculiar blue radiance, as if it were surrounded by the air from above, through which the blue sky shone, instead of the dark depths of the sea. In calm weather the sun could be seen, looking like a purple flower, with the light streaming from the calyx. Each of the young princesses had a little plot of ground in the garden, where she might dig and plant as she pleased. One arranged her flower bed into the form of a whale, another thought it better to make hers like the figure of a little mermaid, but that of the youngest was round like the sun and contained flowers as red as his rays at sunset. She was a strange child, quiet and thoughtful, and while her sisters would be delighted with the wonderful things that they obtained from the wreckage of vessels, she cared for nothing but her pretty red flowers like the sun, except a beautiful marble statue. It was the representation of a handsome boy, carved out of pure white stone, which had fallen to the bottom of the sea from a wreck. She planted by the statue a rose-colored weeping willow. It grew splendidly, and very soon hung its fresh branches over the statue, almost down to the blue sands. The shadow had a violet tint, and waved to and fro like the branches; it seemed as if the crown of the tree and the root were at play and trying to kiss each other. Nothing gave her so much pleasure as to hear about the world above the sea. She made her old grandmother tell her all she knew of the ships and of the towns, the people and the animals. To her it seemed most wonderful and beautiful to hear that the flowers of the land should have fragrance and not those below the sea; that the trees of the forest should be green; and that the fishes among the trees could sing so sweetly, that it was quite a pleasure to hear them. Her grandmother called the little birds fishes, or she would not have understood her, for she had never seen birds.

"When you have reached your fifteenth year," said the grandmother, "you will have permission to rise up out of the sea, to sit on the rocks in the moonlight, while the great ships are sailing by, and then you will see both forests and towns."

In the following year, one of the sisters would be fifteen: But as each was a year younger than the other, the youngest would have to wait five years before her turn came to rise up from the bottom of the ocean and see the earth as we do. However, each promised to tell the others what she saw on her first visit, and what she thought the most beautiful, for their grandmother could not tell them enough; there were so many things on which they wanted information. None of them longed so much for her turn to come as the youngest, she who had the longest time to wait, and who was so quiet and thoughtful. Many nights she stood by the open window, looking up through the dark blue water and watching the fish as they splashed about with their fins and tails. She could see the moon and stars shining faintly, but through the water they looked larger than they do to our eyes. When something like a black cloud passed between her and them, she knew that it was either a whale swimming over her head, or a ship full of human beings, who never imagined that a pretty little mermaid was standing beneath them, holding out her white hands toward the keel of their ship.

As soon as the eldest was fifteen, she was allowed to rise to the surface of the ocean. When she came back, she had hundreds of things to talk about, but the most beautiful, she said, was to lie in the moonlight, on a sandbank, in the quiet sea, near the coast, and to gaze on a large town nearby, where the lights were twinkling like hundreds of stars; to listen to the sounds of the music, the noise of carriages, and the voices of human beings, and then to hear the merry bells peal out from the church steeples; and because she could not go near to all those wonderful things, she longed for them more than ever. Oh, did not the youngest sister listen eagerly to all these descriptions? And afterward, when she stood at the open window looking up through the dark blue water, she thought of the great city, with all its bustle and noise, and even fancied she could hear the sound of the church bells, down in the depths of the sea.

In another year the second sister received permission to rise to the surface of the water and to swim about where she pleased. She rose just as the sun was setting, and, this she said, was the most beautiful sight of all. The whole sky looked like gold, while violet and rose-colored clouds, which she could not describe, floated over her; and, still more rapidly than the clouds, flew a large flock of wild swans toward the setting sun, looking like a long white veil across the sea. She also swam toward the sun, but it sank into the waves, and the rosy tints faded from the clouds and from the sea.

The third sister's turn followed; she was the boldest of them all, and she swam up a broad river that emptied itself into the sea. On the banks she saw green hills covered with beautiful vines; palaces and castles peeped out from amid the proud trees of the forest; she heard the birds singing, and the rays of the sun were so powerful that she was obliged often to dive down under the water to cool her burning face. In a narrow creek she found a whole troop of little human children, quite naked, and sporting about in the water; she wanted to play with them, but they fled in a great fright; and then a little black animal came to the water; it was a dog, but she did not know that, for she had never before seen one. This animal barked at her so terribly that she became frightened and rushed back to the open sea. But she said she should never forget the beautiful forest, the green hills, and the pretty little children who could swim in the water, although they had not fish's tails.

The fourth sister was more timid; she remained in the midst of the sea, but she said it was quite as beautiful there as nearer the land. She could see for so many miles around her, and the sky above looked like a bell of glass. She had seen the ships, but at such a great distance that they looked like seagulls. The dolphins sported in the waves, and the great whales spouted water from their blowholes till it seemed as if a hundred fountains were playing in every direction.

The fifth sister's birthday occurred in the winter, so when her turn came she saw what the others had not seen the first time they went up. The sea looked quite green, and large icebergs were floating about, each like a pearl, she said, but larger and loftier than the churches built by men. They were of the most singular shapes, and glittered like diamonds. She had seated herself upon one of the largest and let the wind play with her long hair, and she remarked that all the ships sailed by rapidly and steered as far away as they could from the iceberg, as if they were afraid of it. Toward evening, as the sun went down, dark clouds covered the sky, the thunder rolled and the lightning flashed, and the red light glowed on the icebergs as they rocked and tossed on the heaving sea. On all the ships, the sails were reefed with fear and trembling, while she sat calmly on the floating iceberg, watching the blue lightning as it darted its forked flashes into the sea.

When first the sisters had permission to rise to the surface, they were each delighted with the new and beautiful sights they saw, but now, as grown-up girls, they could go when they pleased, and they had become indifferent about it. They wished themselves back again in the water, and after a month had passed they said it was much more beautiful down below and pleasanter to be at home. Yet, often in the evening hours, the five sisters would twine their arms around one another and rise to the surface in a row. They had more beautiful voices than any human being could have, and before the approach of a storm and when they expected a ship would be lost, they swam before the vessel and sang sweetly of the delights to be found in the depths of the sea, begging the sailors not to fear if they sank to the bottom. But the sailors could not understand the song; they took it for the howling of the storm. And these things were never to be beautiful for them; for if the ship sank, the men were drowned, and their dead bodies alone reached the palace of the Sea King.

When the sisters rose arm-in-arm through the water in this way, their youngest sister would stand quite alone, looking after them, ready to cry, only that the mermaids have no tears, and therefore they suffer more. "Oh, were I but fifteen years old," said she. "I know that I shall love the world up there and all the people who live in it."

At last she reached her fifteenth year. "Well, now, you are grown up," said the old dowager, her grandmother. "So you must let me adorn you like your other sisters." And she placed a wreath of white lilies in her hair, and every flower leaf was half a pearl. Then the old lady ordered eight great oysters to attach themselves to the tail of the princess to show her high rank.

"But they hurt me so," said the little mermaid.

"Pride must suffer pain," replied the old lady. Oh, how gladly she would have shaken off all this grandeur and laid aside the heavy wreath! The red flowers in her own garden would have suited her much better, but she could not help herself: So she said, "Farewell," and rose as lightly as a bubble to the surface of the water. The sun had just set as she raised her head above the waves, but the clouds were tinted with crimson and gold, and through the glimmering twilight beamed the evening star in all its beauty. The sea was calm, and the air mild and fresh. A large ship, with three masts, lay becalmed on the water, with only one sail set; for not a breeze stiffed, and the sailors sat idle on deck or among the rigging. There was music and song on board, and, as darkness came on, a hundred colored lanterns were lighted, as if the flags of all nations waved in the air. The little mermaid swam close to the cabin windows, and now and then, as the waves lifted her up, she could look in through clear glass windowpanes and see a number of well-dressed people within. Among them was a young prince, the most beautiful of all, with large black eyes; he was sixteen years of age, and his birthday was being kept with much rejoicing. The sailors were dancing on deck, but when the prince came out of the cabin, more than a hundred rockets rose in the air, making it as bright as day. The little mermaid was so startled that she dived underwater, and when she again stretched out her head, it appeared as if all the stars of heaven were falling around her. She had never seen such fireworks before. Great suns spurted fire about, splendid fireflies flew into the blue air, and everything was reflected in the clear, calm sea beneath. The ship itself was so brightly illuminated that all the people, and even the smallest rope, could be distinctly and plainly seen. And how handsome the young prince looked, as he pressed the hands of all present and smiled at them, while the music resounded through the clear night air.

It was very late, yet the little mermaid could not take her eyes from the ship, or from the beautiful prince. The colored lanterns had been extinguished, no more rockets rose in the air, and the cannon had ceased firing; but the sea became restless, and a moaning, grumbling sound could be heard beneath the waves: Still the little mermaid remained by the cabin window, rocking up and down on the water, which enabled her to look in. After a while, the sails were quickly unfurled, and the noble ship continued her passage, but soon the waves rose higher, heavy clouds darkened the sky, and lightning appeared in the distance. A dreadful storm was approaching; once more the sails were reefed, and the great ship pursued her flying course over the raging sea. The waves rose mountains high, as if they would have overtopped the mast, but the ship dived like a swan between them and then rose again on their lofty, foaming crests. To the little mermaid this appeared pleasant sport; not so to the sailors. At length the ship groaned and creaked, the thick planks gave way under the lashing of the sea as it broke over the deck, the mainmast snapped asunder like a reed, the ship lay over on her side, and the water rushed in. The little mermaid now perceived that the crew was in danger; even she herself was obliged to be careful to avoid the beams and planks of the wreck which lay scattered on the water. At one moment it was so pitch dark that she could not see a single object, but a flash of lightning revealed the whole scene. She could see everyone who had been on board except the prince. When the ship parted, she had seen him sink into the deep waves, and she was glad, for she thought he would now be with her; and then she remembered that human beings could not live in the water, so that when he got down to her father's palace he would be quite dead. But he must not die. So she swam about among the beams and planks that strewed the surface of the sea, forgetting that they could crush her to pieces. Then she dived deeply under the dark waters, rising and falling with the waves, till at length she managed to reach the young prince, who was fast losing the power of swimming in that stormy sea. His limbs were failing him, his beautiful eyes were closed, and he would have died had not the little mermaid come to his assistance. She held his head above the water and let the waves drift them where they would.

In the morning the storm had ceased, but of the ship not a single fragment could be seen. The sun rose up red and glowing from the water, and its beams brought back the hue of health to the prince's cheeks, but his eyes remained closed. The mermaid kissed his high, smooth forehead and stroked back his wet hair; he seemed to her like the marble statue in her little garden, and she kissed him again and wished that he might live. Presently they came in sight of land; she saw lofty blue mountains on which the white snow rested as if a flock of swans were lying upon them. Near the coast were beautiful green forests, and close by stood a large building, whether a church or a convent she could not tell. Orange and citron trees grew in the garden, and before the door stood lofty palms. The sea here formed a little bay in which the water was quite still but very deep, so she swam with the handsome prince to the beach, which was covered with fine, white sand, and there she laid him in the warm sunshine, taking care to raise his head higher than his body. Then bells sounded in the large white building, and a number of young girls came into the garden. The little mermaid swam out farther from the shore and placed herself between some high rocks that rose out of the water, then she covered her head and neck with the foam of the sea so that her little face might not be seen and watched to see what would become of the poor prince. She did not wait long before she saw a young girl approach the spot where he lay. She seemed frightened at first, but only for a moment; then she fetched a number of people, and the mermaid saw that the prince came to life again and smiled upon those who stood around him. But to her he sent no smile; he knew not that she had saved him. This made her very unhappy, and when he was led away into the great building, she dived down sorrowfully into the water and returned to her father's castle. She had always been silent and thoughtful, and now she was more so than ever. Her sisters asked her what she had seen during her first visit to the surface of the water, but she would tell them nothing. Many an evening and morning did she rise to the place where she had left the prince. She saw the fruits in the garden ripen till they were gathered, the snow on the tops of the mountains melt away; but she never saw the prince, and therefore she returned home, always more sorrowful than before. It was her only comfort to sit in her own little garden and fling her arm around the beautiful marble statue which was like the prince; but she gave up tending her flowers, and they grew in wild confusion over the paths, twining their long leaves and stems around the branches of the trees so that the whole place became dark and gloomy. At length she could bear it no longer and told one of her sisters all about it. Then the others heard the secret, and very soon it became known to two mermaids whose intimate friend happened to know who the prince was. She had also seen the festival on board ship, and she told them where the prince came from and where his palace stood.

"Come, little sister," said the other princesses; then they entwined their arms and rose up in a long row to the surface of the water, close by the spot where they knew the prince's palace stood. It was built of bright yellow shining stone, with long flights of marble steps, one of which reached quite down to the sea. Splendid gilded cupolas rose over the roof, and between the pillars that surrounded the whole building stood lifelike statues of marble. Through the clear crystal of the lofty windows could be seen noble rooms with costly silk curtains and hangings of tapestry, while the walls were covered with beautiful paintings, which were a pleasure to look at. In the center of the largest saloon, a fountain threw its sparkling jets high up into the glass cupola of the ceiling, through which the sun shone down upon the water and upon the beautiful plants growing around the basin of the fountain. Now that she knew where he lived, she spent many an evening and many a night on the water near the palace. She would swim much nearer the shore than any of the others ventured to do; indeed once she went quite up the narrow channel under the marble balcony, which threw a broad shadow on the water. Here she would sit and watch the young prince, who thought himself quite alone in the bright moonlight. She saw him many times of an evening sailing in a pleasant boat, with music playing and flags waving. She peeped out from among the green rushes, and if the wind caught her long silvery-white veil, those who saw it believed it to be a swan, spreading out its wings. On many a night, too, when the fishermen, with their torches, were out at sea, she heard them relate so many good things about the doings of the young prince that she was glad she had saved his life when he had been tossed about half-dead on the waves. And she remembered that his head had rested on her bosom, and how heartily she had kissed him; but he knew nothing of all this, and could not even dream of her. She grew more and more fond of human beings, and wished more and more to be able to wander about with those whose world seemed to be so much larger than her own. They could fly over the sea in ships, and mount the high hills, which were far above the clouds; and the lands they possessed, their woods and their fields stretched far away beyond the reach of her sight. There was so much that she wished to know, and her sisters were unable to answer all her questions. Then she applied to her old grandmother, who knew all about the upper world, which she very rightly called the lands above the sea.

"If human beings are not drowned," asked the little mermaid, "can they live forever? Do they never die as we do here in the sea?"

"Yes," replied the old lady, "they must also die, and their term of life is even shorter than ours. We sometimes live to three hundred years, but when we cease to exist here we only become the foam on the surface of the water, and we have not even a grave down here of those we love. We have not immortal souls, we shall never live again; but, like the green seaweed, when once it has been cut off, we can never flourish more. Human beings, on the contrary, have a soul that lives forever, lives after the body has been turned to dust. It rises up through the clear, pure air beyond the glittering stars. As we rise out of the water, and behold all the land of the earth, so do they rise to unknown and glorious regions that we shall never see."

"Why have not we an immortal soul?" asked the little mermaid mournfully. "I would give gladly all the hundreds of years that I have to live to be a human being only for one day, and to have the hope of knowing the happiness of that glorious world above the stars."

"You must not think of that," said the old woman. "We feel ourselves to be much happier and much better off than human beings."

"So I shall die," said the little mermaid, "and as the foam of the sea I shall be driven about never again to hear the music of the waves or to see the pretty flowers nor the red sun. Is there anything I can do to win an immortal soul?"

"No," said the old woman. "Unless a man were to love you so much that you were more to him than his father or mother; and if all his thoughts and all his love were fixed upon you, and the priest placed his right hand in yours, and he promised to be true to you here and here-after, then his soul would glide into your body and you would obtain a share in the future happiness of mankind. He would give a soul to you and retain his own as well, but this can never happen. Your fish's tail, which among us is considered so beautiful, is thought on earth to be quite ugly; they do not know any better, and they think it necessary to have two stout props, which they call legs, in order to be handsome."

Then the little mermaid sighed and looked

sorrowfully at her fish's tail. "Let us be happy," said the old lady, "and dart and spring about during the three hundred years that we have to live, which is really quite long enough; after that we can rest ourselves all the better. This evening we are going to have a court ball."

It is one of those splendid sights, which we can never see on earth. The walls and the ceiling of the large ballroom were of thick, but transparent, crystal. Many hundreds of colossal shells, some of a deep red, others of a grass green, stood on each side in rows, with blue fire in them, which lighted up the whole saloon, and shone through the walls, so that the sea was also illuminated. Innumerable fishes, great and small, swam past the crystal walls; on some of them the scales glowed with a purple brilliancy, and on others they shone like silver and gold. Through the halls flowed a broad stream, and in it danced the mermen and the mermaids to the music of their own sweet singing. No one on earth has such a lovely voice as theirs. The little mermaid sang more sweetly than them all. The whole court applauded her with hands and tails; and for a moment her heart felt quite joyful, for she knew she had the loveliest voice of any on earth or in the sea. But she soon thought again of the world above her, for she could not forget the charming prince, nor her sorrow that she had not an immortal soul like his; therefore she crept away silently out of her father's palace, and while everything within was gladness and song, she sat in her own little garden sorrowful and alone. Then she heard the bugle sounding through the water, and thought—*He is certainly sailing above, he on whom my wishes depend, and in whose hands I should like to place the happiness of my life. I will venture all for him, and to win an immortal soul, while my sisters are dancing in my father's palace, I will go to the sea witch, of whom I have always been so much afraid, but she can give me counsel and help.*

And then the little mermaid went out from her garden and took the road to the foaming whirlpools, behind which the sorceress lived. She had never been that way before: Neither flowers nor grass grew there; nothing but bare, gray, sandy ground stretched out to the whirlpool, where the water, like foaming mill-wheels, whirled around everything that it seized, and cast it into the fathomless deep. Through the midst of these crushing whirlpools the little mermaid was obliged to pass, to reach the dominions of the sea witch; and also for a long distance the only road lay right across a quantity of warm, bubbling mire. Beyond this stood the sea witch's house, in the center of a strange forest, in which all the trees and flowers were polypi, half animals and half plants; they looked like serpents with a hundred heads growing out of the ground. The branches were long slimy arms, with fingers like flexible worms, moving limb after limb from the root to the tip. All that could be reached in the sea they seized upon, and held fast, so that it never escaped from their clutches. The little mermaid was so alarmed at what she saw that she stood still, and her heart beat with fear, and she was very nearly turning back; but she thought of the prince, and of the human soul for which she longed, and her courage returned. She fastened her long flowing hair around her head, so that the polypi might not seize hold of it. She laid her hands together across her bosom, and then she darted forward as a fish shoots through the water, between the supple arms and fingers of the ugly polypi, which were stretched out on each side of her. She saw that each held in its grasp something it had seized with its numerous little arms, as if they were iron bands. The white skeletons of human beings who had perished at sea and had sunk down into the deep waters, skeletons of land animals, oars, rudders, and chests of ships were lying tightly grasped by their clinging arms; even a little mermaid whom they had caught and strangled; and this seemed the most shocking of all to the little princess.

She now came to a space of marshy ground in the wood, where large, fat water snakes were rolling in the mire, and showing their ugly, drab-colored bodies. In the midst of this spot stood a house, built with the bones of shipwrecked human beings. There sat the sea witch, allowing a toad to eat from her mouth, just as people sometimes feed a canary with a piece of sugar. She called the ugly water snakes her little chickens, and allowed them to crawl all over her bosom.

"I know what you want," said the sea witch. "It is very stupid of you, but you shall have your way, and it will bring you to sorrow, my pretty princess. You want to get rid of your fish's tail and to have two supports instead of it, like human beings on earth, so that the young prince may fall in love with you, and that you may have an immortal soul." And then the witch laughed so loud and disgustingly that the toad and the snakes fell to the ground and lay there wriggling about. "You are but just in time," said the witch. "For after sunrise tomorrow I should not be able to help you till the end of another year. I will prepare a draft for you, with which you must swim to land tomorrow before sunrise, and sit down on the shore and drink it. Your tail will then disappear and shrink up into what mankind calls legs, and you will feel great pain, as if a sword were passing through you. But all who see you will say that you are the prettiest little human being they ever saw. You will still have the same floating gracefulness of movement, and no dancer will ever tread so lightly, but at every step you take it will feel as if you were treading upon sharp knives and that the blood must flow. If you will bear all this, I will help you."

"Yes, I will," said the little princess in a trembling voice, as she thought of the prince and the immortal soul.

"But think again," said the witch, "for when once your shape has become like a human being, you can no more be a mermaid. You will never return through the water to your sisters or to your father's palace again; and if you do not win the love of the prince, so that he is willing to forget his father and mother for your sake and to love you with his whole soul and allow the priest to join your hands that you may be man and wife, then you will never have an immortal soul. The first morning after he marries another your heart will break, and you will become foam on the crest of the waves."

"I will do it," said the little mermaid, and she became pale as death.

"But I must be paid also," said the witch, "and it is not a trifle that I ask. You have the sweetest voice of any who dwell here in the depths of the sea, and you believe that you will be able to charm the prince with it also, but this voice you must give to me; the best thing you possess will

I have for the price of my draft. My own blood must be mixed with it, that it may be as sharp as a two-edged sword."

"But if you take away my voice," said the little mermaid, "what is left for me?"

"Your beautiful form, your graceful walk, and your expressive eyes; surely with these you can enchain a man's heart. Well, have you lost your courage? Put out your little tongue that I may cut it off as my payment; then you shall have the powerful draft."

"It shall be," said the little mermaid.

Then the witch placed her cauldron on the fire, to prepare the magic draft.

"Cleanliness is a good thing," said she, scouring the vessel with snakes, which she had tied together in a large knot; then she pricked herself in the breast and let the black blood drop into it. The steam that rose formed itself into such horrible shapes that no one could look at them without fear. Every moment the witch threw something else into the vessel, and when it began to boil, the sound was like the weeping of a crocodile. When at last the magic draft was ready, it looked like the clearest water. "There it is for you," said the witch. Then she cut off the mermaid's tongue so that she became mute, and would never again speak or sing. "If the polypi should seize hold of you as you return through the wood," said the witch, "throw over them a few drops of the potion, and their fingers will be torn into a thousand pieces." But the little mermaid had no occasion to do this, for the polypi sprang back in terror when they caught sight of the glittering draft, which shone in her hand like a twinkling star.

So she passed quickly through the wood and the marsh and between the rushing whirlpools. She saw that in her father's palace the torches in the ballroom were extinguished and all within asleep, but she did not venture to go into them, for now she was dumb and going to leave them forever, she felt as if her heart would break. She stole into the garden, took a flower from the flower beds of each of her sisters, kissed her hand a thousand times toward the palace, and then rose up through the dark-blue waters. The sun had not risen when she came in sight of the prince's palace and approached the beautiful marble steps, but the moon shone clear and bright. Then the little mermaid drank the magic draft, and it seemed as if a two-edged sword went through her delicate body. She fell into a swoon and lay like one dead. When the sun arose and shone over the sea, she recovered and felt a sharp pain, but just before her stood the handsome young prince. He fixed his coal-black eyes upon her so earnestly that she cast down her own, and then became aware that her fish's tail was gone, and that she had as pretty a pair of white legs and tiny feet as any little maiden could have; but she had no clothes, so she wrapped herself in her long, thick hair. The prince asked her who she was and where she came from, and she looked at him mildly and sorrowfully with her deep-blue eyes, but she could not speak. Every step she took was as the witch had said it would be. She felt as if treading upon the points of needles or sharp knives, but she bore it willingly and stepped as lightly by the prince's side as a soap bubble, so that he and all who saw her wondered at her graceful swaying movements. She was very soon arrayed in costly robes of silk and muslin, and was the most beautiful creature in the palace, but she was voiceless, and could neither speak nor sing.

Beautiful female servants, dressed in silk and gold, stepped forward and sang before the prince and his royal parents: One sang better than all the others, and the prince clapped his hands and smiled at her. This was great sorrow to the little mermaid; she knew how much more sweetly she herself could sing once, and she thought, *Oh if he could only know that! I have given away my voice forever, to be with him.*

The servants next performed some pretty fairy-like dances to the sound of beautiful music. Then the little mermaid raised her lovely white arms, stood on the tips of her toes, and glided over the floor, dancing as no one yet had been able to dance. At each moment her beauty became more revealed, and her expressive eyes appealed more directly to the heart than the songs of the servants. Everyone was enchanted, especially the prince, who called her his little foundling; and she danced again quite readily, to please him, though each time her foot touched the floor it seemed as if she trod on sharp knives.

The prince said she should remain with him always, and she received permission to sleep at his door, on a velvet cushion. He had a page's dress made for her, that she might accompany him on horseback. They rode together through the sweet-scented woods, where the green boughs touched their shoulders, and the little birds sang among the fresh leaves. She climbed with the prince to the tops of high mountains, and although her tender feet bled so that even her steps were marked, she only laughed and followed him till they could see the clouds beneath them looking like a flock of birds traveling to distant lands. While at the prince's palace, and when all the household was asleep, she would go and sit on the broad marble steps, for it eased her burning feet to bathe them in the cold seawater, and then she thought of all those below in the deep.

Once during the night, her sisters came up arm-in-arm, singing sorrowfully, as they floated on the water. She beckoned to them, and then they recognized her and told her how she had grieved them. After that, they came to the same place every night, and once she saw in the distance her old grandmother, who had not been to the surface of the sea for many years, and the old Sea King, her father, with his crown on his head. They stretched out their hands toward her, but they did not venture so near the land as her sisters did.

As the days passed, she loved the prince more fondly, and he loved her as he would love a little child, but it never came into his head to make her his wife; yet, unless he married her, she could not receive an immortal soul; and, on the morning after his marriage with another, she would dissolve into the foam of the sea.

"Do you not love me the best of them all?" the eyes of the little mermaid seemed to say, when he took her in his arms and kissed her fair forehead.

"Yes, you are dear to me," said the prince. "For you have the best heart, and you are the most devoted to me; you are like a young maiden whom I once saw, but whom I shall never meet again. I was in a ship that was wrecked, and the waves cast me ashore near a holy temple, where several young maidens performed the service. The youngest of them found me on the shore and saved my life. I saw her but twice, and she is the only one in the world whom I could love; but you are like her, and you have almost driven her image out of my mind. She belongs to the holy temple, and my good fortune has sent you to me instead of her, and we will never part."

Ah, he knows not that it was I who saved his life, thought the little mermaid. *I carried him over the sea to the wood where the temple stands. I sat beneath the foam and watched till the human beings came to help him. I saw the pretty maiden that he loves better than he loves me*, and the mermaid sighed deeply, but she could not shed tears. *He says the maiden belongs to the holy temple, therefore she will never return to the world. They will meet no more while I am by his side and see him every day. I will take care of him and love him and give up my life for his sake.*

Very soon it was said that the prince must marry, and that the beautiful daughter of a neighboring king would be his wife, for a fine ship was being fitted out. Although the prince gave out that he merely intended to pay a visit to the king, it was generally supposed that he really went to see his daughter. A great company were to go with him. The little mermaid smiled and shook her head. She knew the prince's thoughts better than any of the others.

"I must travel," he had said to her. "I must see this beautiful princess; my parents desire it, but they will not oblige me to bring her home as my bride. I cannot love her; she is not like the beautiful maiden in the temple whom you resemble. If I were forced to choose a bride, I would rather choose you, my silent beauty, with those expressive eyes." And then he kissed her rosy mouth, played with her long waving hair, and laid his head on her heart while she dreamed of human happiness and an immortal soul. "You are not afraid of the sea," said he, as they stood on the deck of the noble ship that was to carry them to the country of the neighboring king. And then he told her of storm and of calm, of strange fishes in the deep beneath them and of what the divers had seen there, and she smiled at his descriptions, for she knew better than anyone what wonders were at the bottom of the sea.

In the moonlight, when all on board were asleep, except the man at the helm who was steering, she sat on the deck, gazing down through the clear water. She thought she could distinguish her father's castle, and upon it her aged grandmother with the silver crown on her head, looking through the rushing tide at the keel of the vessel. Then her sisters came up on the waves and gazed at her mournfully, wringing their white hands. She beckoned to them and smiled, and wanted to tell them how happy and well off she was, but the cabin boy approached, and when her sisters dived down he thought it was only the foam of the sea that he saw.

The next morning the ship sailed into the harbor of a beautiful town belonging to the king whom the prince was going to visit. The church bells were ringing, and from the high towers sounded a flourish of trumpets; and soldiers, with flying colors and glittering bayonets, lined the rocks through which they passed. Every day was a festival; balls and entertainments followed one another.

But the princess had not yet appeared. People said that she was being brought up and educated in a religious house where she was learning every royal virtue. At last she came. Then the little mermaid, who was very anxious to see whether she was really beautiful, was obliged to acknowledge that she had never seen a more perfect vision of beauty. Her skin was delicately fair, and beneath her long dark eyelashes her laughing blue eyes shone with truth and purity.

"It was you," said the prince, "who saved my life when I lay dead on the beach," and he folded his blushing bride in his arms. "Oh, I am too happy," said he to the little mermaid. "My fondest hopes are all fulfilled. You will rejoice at my happiness; for your devotion to me is great and sincere."

The little mermaid kissed his hand and felt as if her heart were already broken. His wedding morning would bring death to her, and she would change into the foam of the sea. All the church bells rang, and the heralds rode about the town proclaiming the betrothal. Perfumed oil was burning in costly silver lamps on every altar. The priests waved the censers, while the bride and bridegroom joined their hands and received the blessing of the bishop. The little mermaid, dressed in silk and gold, held up the bride's train, but her ears heard nothing of the festive music, and her eyes saw not the holy ceremony; she thought of the night of death that was coming to her, and of all she had lost in the world. On the same evening the bride and bridegroom went on board ship; cannons were roaring, flags waving, and in the center of the ship a costly tent of purple and gold had been erected. It contained elegant couches for the reception of the bridal pair during the night. The ship, with swelling sails and a favorable wind, glided away smoothly and lightly over the calm sea. When it grew dark, a number of colored lamps were lighted, and the sailors danced merrily on the deck. The little mermaid could not help thinking of her first rising out of the sea, when she had seen similar festivities and joys, and she joined in the dance, poised herself in the air as a swallow when he pursues his prey, and all present cheered her with wonder. She had never danced so elegantly before. Her tender feet felt as if cut with sharp knives, but she cared not for it; a sharper pang had pierced through her heart.

She knew this was the last evening she should ever see the prince, for whom she had forsaken her kindred and her home; she had given up her beautiful voice, and suffered unheard-of pain daily for him while he knew nothing of it. This was the last evening that she would breathe the same air with him or gaze on the starry sky and the deep sea; an eternal night, without a thought or a dream, awaited her: She had no soul and now she could never win one. All was joy and laughter on board ship till long after midnight; she laughed and danced with the rest, while the thoughts of death were in her heart. The prince kissed his beautiful bride, while she played with his raven hair, till they went arm-in-arm to rest in the splendid tent. Then all became still on board the ship; the helmsman, alone awake, stood at the helm. The little mermaid leaned her white arms on the edge of the vessel and looked toward the east for the first blush of morning, for that first ray of dawn that would bring her death. She saw her sisters rising out of the flood: They were as pale as herself, but their long beautiful hair waved no more in the wind and had been cut off.

"We have given our hair to the witch," said they, "to obtain help for you, that you may not die tonight. She has given us a knife. Here it is, see it is very sharp. Before the sun rises you must plunge it into the heart of the prince. When the warm blood falls upon your feet they will grow together again and form into a fish's tail, and you will be once more a mermaid and return to us to live out your three hundred years before you die and change into the salt sea foam. Haste, then. He or you must die before sunrise. Our old grandmother moans so for you that her white hair is falling off from sorrow, as ours fell under the witch's scissors. Kill the prince and come back. Hasten. Do you not see the first red streaks in the sky?

In a few minutes the sun will rise, and you must die."
And then they sighed deeply and mournfully, and sank
down beneath the waves.

The little mermaid drew back the crimson curtain of
the tent, and beheld the fair bride with her head resting
on the prince's breast. She bent down and kissed his fair
brow, then looked at the sky on which the rosy dawn
grew brighter and brighter; then she glanced at the sharp
knife, and again fixed her eyes on the prince, who whispered the name of his bride in his dreams. She was in his
thoughts, and the knife trembled in the hand of the little
mermaid. Then she flung it far away from her into the
waves, the water turned red where it fell, and the drops
that spurted up looked like blood. She cast one more lin-
gering, half-fainting glance at the prince, and then threw
herself from the ship into the sea and thought her body
was dissolving into foam. The sun rose above the waves,
and his warm rays fell on the cold foam of the little

mermaid, who did not feel as if she were dying. She saw the bright sun, and all around her floated hundreds of transparent beautiful beings; she could see through them the white sails of the ship and the red clouds in the sky; their speech was melodious, but too ethereal to be heard by mortal ears, as they were also unseen by mortal eyes. The little mermaid perceived that she had a body like theirs, and that she continued to rise higher and higher out of the foam. "Where am I?" asked she, and her voice sounded ethereal, as the voice of those who were with her; no earthly music could imitate it.

"Among the daughters of the air," answered one of them. "A mermaid has not an immortal soul, nor can she obtain one unless she wins the love of a human being. On the power of another hangs her eternal destiny. But the daughters of the air, although they do not possess an immortal soul, can, by their good deeds, procure one for themselves. We fly to warm countries and cool the sultry air that destroys mankind with the pestilence. We carry the perfume of the flowers to spread health and restoration. After we have striven for three hundred years to all the good in our power, we receive an immortal soul and take part in the happiness of mankind. You, poor little mermaid, have tried with your whole heart to do as we are doing. You have suffered and endured and raised yourself to the spirit world by your good deeds, and now, by striving for three hundred years in the same way, you may obtain an immortal soul."

The little mermaid lifted her glorified eyes toward the sun, and felt them, for the first time, filling with tears. On the ship, in which she had left the prince, there was life and noise. She saw him and his beautiful bride searching for her. Sorrowfully they gazed at the pearly foam, as if they knew she had thrown herself into the waves. Unseen, she kissed the forehead of the bride and fanned the prince, and then mounted with the other children of the air to a rosy cloud that floated through the ether.

"After three hundred years, thus shall we float into the kingdom of heaven," said she. "And we may even get there sooner," whispered one of her companions. "Unseen, we can enter the houses of men, where there are children, and for every day on which we find a good child, who is the joy of his parents and deserves their love, our time of probation is shortened. The child does not know when we fly through the room, that we smile with joy at his good conduct, for we can count one year less of our three hundred years. But when we see a naughty or a wicked child, we shed tears of sorrow, and for every tear a day is added to our time of trial!"

Holger Danske

In Denmark there stands an old castle named Kronenburg, close by the Sound of Elsinore, where large ships, English, Russian, and Prussian, pass by hundreds every day. And they salute the old castle with cannons, "Boom, boom," which is as if they said, "Good day." And the cannons of the old castle answer "Boom," which means "Many thanks." In winter no ships sail by, for the whole Sound is covered with ice as far as the Swedish coast, and has quite the appearance of a main road. The Danish and the Swedish flags wave, and Danes and Swedes say, "Good day," and "Thank you" to each other, not with cannons, but with a friendly shake of the hand; and they exchange white bread and biscuits with each other, because foreign articles taste the best.

But the most beautiful sight of all is the old castle of Kronenburg, where Holger Danske sits in the deep, dark cellar into which no one goes. He is clad in iron and steel, and rests his head on his strong arm; his long beard hangs down upon the marble table, into which it has become firmly rooted; he sleeps and dreams, but in his dreams he sees everything that happens in Denmark. On each Christmas Eve an angel comes to him and tells him that all he has dreamed is true, and that he may go to sleep again in peace, as Denmark is not yet in any real danger; but should danger ever come, then Holger Danske will rouse himself, and the table will burst asunder as he draws out his beard. Then he will come forth in his strength and strike a blow that shall sound in all the countries of the world.

An old grandfather sat and told his little grandson all this about Holger Danske, and the boy knew that what his grandfather told him must be true. As the old man related this story, he was carving an image in wood to represent Holger Danske, to be fastened to the prow of a ship; for the old grandfather was a carver in wood, that is, one who carved figures for the heads of ships according to the names given to them. And now he had carved Holger Danske, who stood there erect and proud, with his long beard, holding in one hand his broad battle-ax, while with the other he leaned on the Danish arms. The old grandfather told the little boy a great deal about Danish men and women who had distinguished themselves in olden times, so that he fancied he knew as much even as Holger Danske himself, who, after all, could only dream; and when the little fellow went to bed, he thought so much about it that he actually pressed his chin against the counterpane and imagined that he had a long beard that had become rooted to it. But the old grandfather remained sitting at his work and carving away at the last part of it, which was the Danish arms.

And when he had finished he looked at the whole figure, and thought of all he had heard and read, and what he had that evening related to his little grandson. Then he nodded his head, wiped his spectacles and put them on, and said, "Ah, yes; Holger Danske will not appear in my lifetime, but the boy who is in bed there may very likely live to see him when the event really comes to pass." And the old grandfather nodded again, and the more he looked at Holger Danske, the more satisfied he felt that he had carved a good image of him. It seemed to glow with the color of life; the armor glittered like iron and steel. The hearts in the Danish arms grew more and more red, while the lions, with gold crowns on their heads, were leaping up. "That is the most beautiful coat of arms in the world," said the old man. "The lions represent strength; and the hearts, gentleness and love." And as he gazed on the uppermost lion, he thought of King Canute, who chained great England to Denmark's throne; and he looked at the second lion and thought of Waldemar, who untied Denmark and conquered the Vandals. The third lion reminded him of Margaret, who united Denmark, Sweden, and Norway. But when he gazed at the red hearts, their colors glowed more deeply, even as flames, and his memory followed each in turn. The first led him to a dark, narrow prison, in which sat a prisoner, a beautiful woman, daughter of Christian the Fourth, Eleanor Ulfeld, and the flame became a rose on her bosom, and its blossoms were not more pure than the heart of this noblest and best of all Danish women. "Ah, yes, that is indeed a noble heart in the Danish arms," said the grandfather, and his spirit followed the second flame, which carried him out to sea, where cannons roared and the ships lay shrouded in smoke, and the flaming heart attached itself to the breast of Hvitfeldt in the form of the ribbon of an order, as he blew himself and his ship into the air in order to save the fleet. And the third flame led him to Greenland's wretched huts, where the preacher, Hans Egede, ruled with love in every word and action. The flame was as a star on his breast and added another heart to the Danish arms. And as the old grandfather's spirit followed the next hovering flame, he knew whereabout it would lead him. In a peasant woman's humble room stood Frederick the Sixth, writing his name with chalk on the beam. The flame trembled on his breast and in his heart, and it was in the peasant's room that his heart became one for the Danish arms. The old grandfather wiped his eyes, for he had known King Frederick, with his silvery locks and his honest blue eyes, and had lived for him, and he folded his hands and remained for some time silent. Then his daughter-in-law came to him and said it was getting late, that he ought to rest for a while, and that the supper was on the table.

"What you have been carving is very beautiful, Grandfather," said she. "Holger Danske and the old coat of arms; it seems to me as if I have seen the face somewhere."

"No, that is impossible," replied the old grandfather, "but I have seen it, and I have tried to carve it in wood, as I have retained it in my memory. It was a long time ago, while the English fleet lay in the roads, on the second of April, when we showed that we were true, ancient Danes. I was onboard the *Denmark*, in Steene Bille's squadron; I had a man by my side whom even the cannonballs seemed to fear. He sung old songs in a merry voice, and fired and fought as if he were something more than a man. I still remember his face, but from whence he came, or whither he went, I know not; no one knows. I have often thought it might have been Holger Danske himself, who had swum down to us from Kronenburg to help us in the hour of danger. That was my idea, and there stands his likeness."

The wooden figure threw a gigantic shadow on the wall, and even on part of the ceiling; it seemed as if the real Holger Danske stood behind it, for the shadow moved; but this was no doubt caused by the flame of the lamp not burning steadily. Then the daughter-in-law kissed the old grandfather, and led him to a large arm-chair by the table; and she, and her husband, who was the son of the old man and the father of the little boy who lay in bed, sat down to supper with him. And the old grand-father talked of the Danish lions and the Danish hearts, emblems of strength and gentleness and explained quite clearly that there is another strength than that which lies in a sword, and he pointed to a shelf where lay a number of old books, and among them a collection of Holberg's plays, which are much read and are so clever and amusing that it is easy to fancy we have known the people of those days, who are described in them.

"He knew how to fight also," said the old man. "For he lashed the follies and prejudices of people during his whole life."

Then the grandfather nodded to a place above the looking glass, where hung an almanac, with a representation of the Round Tower upon it, and said, "Tycho Brahe was another of those who used a sword, but not one to cut into the flesh and bone, but to make the way of the stars of heaven clear and plain to be understood. And then he, whose father belonged to my calling—yes, he, the son of the old image-carver, he whom we ourselves have seen, with his silvery locks and his broad shoulders, whose name is known in all lands—yes, he was a sculptor, while I am only a carver. Holger Danske can appear in marble, so that people in all countries of the world may hear of the strength of Denmark. Now let us drink the health of Bertel."

But the little boy in bed saw plainly the old castle of Kronenburg and the Sound of Elsinore and Holger Danske, far down in the cellar with his beard rooted to the table and dreaming of everything that was passing above him.

And Holger Danske did dream of the little humble room in which the image-carver sat; he heard all that had been said, and he nodded in his dream, saying, "Ah, yes, remember me, you Danish people, keep me in your memory, I will come to you in the hour of need."

The bright morning light shone over Kronenburg, and the wind brought the sound of the hunting horn across from the neighboring shores. The ships sailed by and saluted the castle with the boom of the cannon, and Kronenburg returned the salute, "Boom, boom." But the roaring cannons did not awake Holger Danske, for they meant only "Good morning," and "Thank you." They must fire in another fashion before he awakes; but wake he will, for there is energy yet in Holger Danske.

The Nightingale

In China, you know, the emperor is Chinese, and all those about him are Chinese also. The story I am going to tell you happened a great many years ago, so it is well to hear it now before it is forgotten. The emperor's palace was the most beautiful in the world. It was built entirely of porcelain, and very costly, but so delicate and brittle that whoever touched it was obliged to be careful. In the garden could be seen the most singular flowers, with pretty silver bells tied to them, which tinkled so that everyone who passed could not help noticing the flowers. Indeed, everything in the emperor's garden was remarkable, and it extended so far that the gardener himself did not know where it ended. Those who traveled beyond its limits knew that there was a noble forest, with lofty trees, sloping down to the deep blue sea, and the great ships sailed under the shadow of its branches. In one of these trees lived a nightingale, who sang so beautifully that even the poor fishermen, who had so many other things to do, would stop and listen. Sometimes, when they went at night to spread their nets, they would hear her sing, and say, "Oh, is not that beautiful?" But when they returned to their fishing, they forgot the bird until the next night. Then they would hear it again, and exclaim, "Oh, how beautiful is the nightingale's song!"

Travelers from every country in the world came to the city of the emperor, which they admired very much, as well as the palace and gardens; but when they heard the nightingale, they all declared it to be the best of all. And the travelers, on their return home, related what they had seen; and learned men wrote books, containing descriptions of the town, the palace, and the gardens; but they did not forget the nightingale, which was really the greatest wonder. And those who could write poetry composed beautiful verses about the nightingale, who lived in a forest near the deep sea. The books traveled all over the world, and some of them came into the hands of the emperor; and he sat in his golden chair, and, as he read, he nodded his approval every moment, for it pleased him to find such a beautiful description of his city, his palace, and his gardens. But when he came to the words, *the nightingale is the most beautiful of all*, he exclaimed, "What is this? I know nothing of any nightingale. Is there such a bird in my empire? And even in my garden? I have never heard of it. Something, it appears, may be learnt from books."

Then he called one of his lords-in-waiting, who was so high bred, that when any in an inferior rank to himself spoke to him or asked him a question, he would answer, "Pooh," which means nothing.

"There is a very wonderful bird mentioned here,

called a nightingale," said the emperor. "They say it is the best thing in my large kingdom. Why have I not been told of it?"

"I have never heard the name," replied the cavalier. "She has not been presented at court."

"It is my pleasure that she shall appear this evening," said the emperor. "The whole world knows what I possess better than I do myself."

"I have never heard of her," said the cavalier, "yet I will endeavor to find her."

But where was the nightingale to be found? The nobleman went upstairs and down, through halls and passages; yet none of those whom he met had heard of the bird. So he returned to the emperor, and said that it must be a fable, invented by those who had written the book. "Your Imperial Majesty," said he, "cannot believe everything contained in books; sometimes they are only fiction, or what is called the black art."

"But the book in which I have read this account," said the emperor, "was sent to me by the great and mighty emperor of Japan, and therefore it cannot contain a falsehood. I will hear the nightingale, she must be here this evening. She has my highest favor, and if she does not come, the whole court shall be trampled upon after supper is ended."

"Oh, no!" cried the lord-in-waiting, and again he ran up and downstairs, through all the halls and corridors; and half the court ran with him, for they did not like the idea of being trampled upon. There was a great inquiry about this wonderful nightingale, whom all the world knew, but who was unknown to the court.

At last they met with a poor little girl in the kitchen, who said, "Oh, yes, I know the nightingale quite well; indeed, she can sing. Every evening I have permission to take home to my poor sick mother the scraps from the table; she lives down by the seashore, and as I come back

I feel tired, and I sit down in the wood to rest and listen to the nightingale's song. Then the tears come into my eyes, and it is just as if my mother kissed me."

"Little maiden," said the lord-in-waiting, "I will obtain for you constant employment in the kitchen, and you shall have permission to see the emperor dine, if you will lead us to the nightingale; for she is invited for this evening to the palace." So she went into the wood where the nightingale sang, and half the court followed her. As they went along, a cow began mooing.

"Oh," said a young courtier, "now we have found her; what wonderful power for such a small creature; I have certainly heard it before."

"No, that is only a cow mooing," said the little girl. "We are a long way from the place yet."

Then some frogs began to croak in the marsh.

"Beautiful," said the young courtier again. "Now I hear it, tinkling like little church bells."

"No, those are frogs," said the little maiden, "but I think we shall soon hear her now." And presently the nightingale began to sing.

"Hark, hark! There she is," said the girl, "and there she sits," she added, pointing to a little gray bird who was perched on a bough.

"Is it possible?" said the lord-in-waiting. "I never imagined it would be a little, plain, simple thing like that. She has certainly changed color at seeing so many grand people around her."

"Little nightingale," cried the girl, raising her voice, "our most gracious emperor wishes you to sing before him."

"With the greatest pleasure," said the nightingale, and she began to sing most delightfully.

"It sounds like tiny glass bells," said the lord-in-waiting, "and see how her little throat works. It is surprising that we have never heard this before; she will be a great success at court."

"Shall I sing once more before the emperor?" asked the nightingale, who thought he was present.

"My excellent little nightingale," said the courtier, "I have the great pleasure of inviting you to a court festival this evening, where you will gain imperial favor by your charming song."

"My song sounds best in the green wood," said the bird, but still she came willingly when she heard the emperor's wish.

The palace was elegantly decorated for the occasion. The walls and floors of porcelain glittered in the light of a thousand lamps. Beautiful flowers, around which little bells were tied, stood in the corridors. What with the running to and fro and the draft, these bells tinkled so loudly that no one could speak to be heard. In the center of the great hall, a golden perch had been fixed for the nightingale to sit on. The whole court was present, and the little kitchen maid had received permission to stand by the door. She was not installed as a real court cook. All were in full dress, and every eye was turned to the little gray bird when the emperor nodded to her to begin. The nightingale sang so sweetly that the tears came into the emperor's eyes, and then rolled down his cheeks, as her song became still more touching and went to everyone's heart. The emperor was so delighted that he declared the nightingale should have his gold slipper to wear around her neck, but she declined the honor with thanks: She had been sufficiently rewarded already. "I have seen tears in an emperor's eyes," she said, "that is my richest reward. An emperor's tears have wonderful power, and are quite sufficient honor for me." And then she sang again more enchantingly than ever.

"That singing is a lovely gift," said the ladies of the court to each other, and then they took water in their mouths to make them utter the gurgling sounds of the nightingale when they spoke to anyone, so that they might fancy themselves nightingales. And the footmen and chambermaids also expressed their satisfaction, which is saying a great deal, for they are very difficult to please. In fact the nightingale's visit was most successful. She was now to remain at court, to have her own cage— with liberty to go out twice a day, and once during the night. Twelve servants were appointed to attend her on these occasions, who each held her by a silken string fastened to her leg. There was certainly not much pleasure in this kind of flying.

The whole city spoke of the wonderful bird, and when two people met, one said "nightin," and the other said "gale," and they understood what was meant, for nothing else was talked of. Eleven peddlers' children were named after her, but not one of them could sing a note.

One day the emperor received a large packet on which was written "The Nightingale." "Here is no doubt a new book about our celebrated bird," said the emperor. But instead of a book, it was a work of art contained in a casket, an artificial nightingale made to look like a living one, and covered all over with diamonds, rubies, and sapphires. As soon as the artificial bird was wound up, it could sing like the real one, and could move its tail up and down, which sparkled with silver and gold. Around its neck hung a piece of ribbon, on which was written "The Emperor of China's nightingale is poor compared with that of the Emperor of Japan's."

"This is very beautiful," exclaimed all who saw it, and he who had brought the artificial bird received the title of "Imperial Nightingale-Bringer-in-Chief."

"Now they must sing together," said the court, "and what a duet it will be." But they did not get on well, for the real nightingale sang in its own natural way, but the artificial bird sang only waltzes.

"That is not a fault," said the music master, "it is quite perfect to my taste," so then it had to sing alone, and was as successful as the real bird; besides, it was so much prettier to look at, for it sparkled like bracelets and breastpins. Three and thirty times did it sing the same tunes without being tired; the people would gladly have heard it again, but the emperor said the living nightingale ought to sing something. But where was she? No one had noticed her when she flew out at the open window, back to her own green woods.

"What strange conduct," said the emperor, when her flight had been discovered, all the courtiers blamed her and said she was a very ungrateful creature.

"But we have the best bird after all," said one, and then they would have the bird sing again, although it was the thirty-fourth time they had listened to the same piece, and even then they had not learnt it, for it was rather difficult. But the music master praised the bird in the highest degree, and even asserted that it was better than a real nightingale, not only in its dress and the beautiful diamonds, but also in its musical power. "For you must perceive, my chief lord and emperor, that with a real nightingale we can never tell what is going to be sung, but with this bird everything is settled. It can be opened and explained, so that people may understand how the waltzes are formed, and why one note follows upon another."

"This is exactly what we think," they all replied, and then the music master received permission to exhibit the bird to the people on the following Sunday, and the emperor commanded that they should be present to hear it sing. When they heard it they were like people intoxicated. They all said "Oh!" and held up their forefingers and nodded, but a poor fisherman, who had heard the real nightingale, said, "It sounds prettily enough, and the melodies are all alike; yet there seems something wanting, I cannot exactly tell what."

And after this the real nightingale was banished from

the empire, and the artificial bird placed on a silk cushion close to the emperor's bed. The presents of gold and precious stones that had been received with it were around the bird, and it was now advanced to the title of "Little Imperial Singer," and to the rank of No. 1 on the left hand; for the emperor considered the left side, on which the heart lies, as the most noble, and the heart of an emperor is in the same place as that of other people.

The music master wrote a work, in twenty-five volumes, about the artificial bird, which was very learned and very long, and full of the most difficult Chinese words; yet all the people said they had read it, and understood it, for fear of being thought stupid.

So a year passed, and the emperor, the court, and all the people knew every little turn in the artificial bird's song; and for that same reason it pleased them better. They could sing with the bird, which they often did. The street boys sang, "Zi-zi-zi, cluck, cluck, cluck," and the emperor himself could sing it also. It was really most amusing.

One evening, when the artificial bird was singing its best, and the emperor lay in bed listening to it, something inside the bird sounded *whizz*. Then a spring cracked. *Whir-r-r-r* went all the wheels, running around, and then the music stopped. The emperor immediately sprang out of bed and called for his physician; but what could he do? Then they sent for a watchmaker; and, after a great deal of talking and examination, the bird was put into something like order; but he said that it must be used very carefully, as the barrels were worn, and it would be impossible to put in new ones without injuring the music. Now there was great sorrow, as the bird could only be allowed to play once a year; and even that was dangerous for the works inside it. Then the music master made a little speech, full of hard words, and declared that the bird was as good as ever, and, of course, no one contradicted him.

Five years passed, and then a real grief came upon the land. The people really were fond of their emperor, and he now lay so ill that he was not expected to live. Already a new emperor had been chosen and the people who stood in the street asked the lord-in-waiting how the old emperor was, but he only said, "Pooh!" and shook his head.

Cold and pale lay the emperor in his royal bed; the whole court thought he was dead, and everyone ran away to pay homage to his successor. The chamberlains went out to have a talk on the matter, and the maids invited company to take coffee. Cloth had been laid down on the halls and passages, so that not a footstep should be heard, and all was silent and still. But the emperor was not yet dead, although he lay white and stiff on his gorgeous bed, with the long velvet curtains and heavy gold tassels. A window stood open, and the moon shone in upon the emperor and the artificial bird. The poor emperor, finding he could scarcely breathe with a strange weight on his chest, opened his eyes and saw Death sitting there. He had put on the emperor's golden crown, and held in one hand his sword of state, and in the other his beautiful banner. All around the bed and peeping through the long velvet curtains were a number of strange heads, some very ugly and others lovely and gentle looking. These were the emperor's good and bad deeds, which stared him in the face now that Death sat at his heart.

"Do you remember this?" "Do you recollect that?" they asked one after another, thus bringing to his remembrance circumstances that made the perspiration stand on his brow.

"I know nothing about it," said the emperor. "Music! music!" he cried. "The large drum! that I may not hear what they say." But they still went on, and Death nodded to all they said. "Music! music!" shouted the emperor. "You little precious Golden Bird, sing, pray sing! I have given you gold and costly presents; I have even hung my golden slipper around your neck. Sing! sing!" But the bird remained silent. There was no one to wind it up, and therefore it could not sing a note.

Death continued to stare at the emperor with his cold, hollow eyes, and the room was fearfully still. Suddenly there came through the open window the sound of sweet music. Outside, on the bough of a tree, sat the living nightingale. She had heard of the emperor's illness, and had therefore come to sing to him of hope and trust. And as she sung, the shadows grew paler and paler; the blood in the emperor's veins flowed more rapidly, and gave life to his weak limbs, and even Death himself listened and said, "Go on, little nightingale, go on."

"Then will you give me the beautiful golden sword

and that rich banner? And will you give me the emperor's crown?" said the bird.

So Death gave up each of these treasures for a song; and the nightingale continued her singing. She sung of the quiet churchyard, where the white roses grow, where the elder tree wafts its perfume on the breeze, and the fresh, sweet grass is moistened by the mourners' tears. Then Death longed to go and see his garden, and floated out through the window in the form of a cold, white mist.

"Thanks, thanks, you heavenly little bird. I know you well. I banished you from my kingdom once, and yet you have charmed away the evil faces from my bed and banished Death from my heart with your sweet song. How can I reward you?"

"You have already rewarded me," said the nightingale. "I shall never forget that I drew tears from your eyes the first time I sang to you. These are the jewels that rejoice a singer's heart. But now sleep, and grow strong and well. I will sing to you again."

And as she sung, the emperor fell into a sweet sleep, and how mild and refreshing that slumber was! When he awoke, strengthened and restored, the sun shone brightly through the window, but not one of his servants had returned—they all believed he was dead; only the nightingale still sat beside him, and sang.

"You must always remain with me," said the emperor. "You shall sing only when it pleases you, and I will break the artificial bird into a thousand pieces."

"No; do not do that," replied the nightingale. "The bird did very well as long as it could. Keep it here still. I cannot live in the palace and build my nest, but let me come when I like. I will sit on a bough outside your window in the evening, and sing to you so that you may be happy and have thoughts full of joy. I will sing to you of those who are happy and those who suffer; of the good and the evil, who are hidden around you. The little singing bird flies far from you and your court to the home of the fisherman and the peasant's cot. I love your heart better than your crown; and yet something holy lingers around that also. I will come. I will sing to you, but you must promise me one thing."

"Everything," said the emperor, who, having dressed himself in his imperial robes, stood with the hand that held the heavy golden sword pressed to his heart.

"I ask only one thing," she replied. "Let no one know that you have a little bird who tells you everything. It will be best to conceal it." So saying, the nightingale flew away.

The servants now came in to look after the dead emperor; when, lo! there he stood, and, to their astonishment, said, "Good morning."

The Snow Queen

In Seven Stories

First Story

Which Describes a Looking Glass and the Broken Fragments

You must attend to the commencement of this story, for when we get to the end we shall know more than we do now about a very wicked hobgoblin; he was one of the very worst, for he was a real demon. One day, when he was in a merry mood, he made a looking glass that had the power of making everything good or beautiful that was reflected in it almost shrink to nothing, while everything that was worthless and bad looked increased in size and worse than ever. The most lovely landscapes appeared like boiled spinach, and the people became hideous, and looked as if they stood on their heads and had no bodies. Their countenances were so distorted that no one could recognize them, and even one freckle on the face appeared to spread over the whole of the nose and mouth. The demon said this was very amusing. When a good or pious thought passed through the mind of anyone it was misrepresented in the glass; and then how the demon laughed at his cunning invention. All who went to the demon's school—for he kept a school—talked everywhere of the wonders they had seen and declared that people could now, for the first time, see what the world and mankind were really like. They carried the glass about everywhere, till at last there was not a land nor a people who had not been looked at through this distorted mirror. They wanted even to fly with it up to heaven to see the angels, but the higher they flew the more slippery the glass became, and they could scarcely hold it, till at last it slipped from their hands, fell to the earth, and was broken into millions of pieces. But now the looking glass caused more unhappiness than ever, for some of the fragments were not so large as a grain of sand, and they flew about the world into every country. When one of these tiny atoms flew into a person's eye, it stuck there unknown to him, and from that moment he saw everything through a distorted medium, or could see only the worst side of what he looked at, for even the smallest fragment retained the same power that had belonged to the whole mirror. Some few persons even got a fragment of the looking glass in their hearts, and this was very terrible, for their hearts became cold like a lump of ice. A few of the pieces were so large that they could be used as windowpanes; it would have been a sad thing to look at our friends through them. Other pieces were made into spectacles; this was dreadful for those who wore them, for they could see nothing either rightly or justly. At all this the wicked demon laughed till his sides shook—it tickled him so to see the mischief he had done. There were still a number of these little fragments of glass floating about in the air, and now you shall hear what happened with one of them.

Second Story

A Little Boy and a Little Girl

In a large town, full of houses and people, there is not room for everybody to have even a little garden; therefore they are obliged to be satisfied with a few flowers in flowerpots. In one of these large towns lived two poor children who had a garden something larger and better than a few pots. They were not brother and sister, but they loved each other almost as much as if they had been. Their parents lived opposite to each other in two garrets, where the roofs of neighboring houses projected out toward each other and the water pipe ran between them. In each house was a little window, so that anyone could step across the gutter from one window to the other. The parents of these children had each a large wooden box in which they cultivated kitchen herbs for their own use, and a little rosebush in each box, which grew splendidly. Now after a while the parents decided to place these two boxes across the water pipe, so that they reached from one window to the other and looked like two banks of flowers. Sweet peas drooped over the boxes, and the roses shot forth long branches, which were trained around the windows and clustered together almost like a triumphal arch of leaves and flowers. The boxes were very high, and the children knew they must not climb upon them, without permission, but they were often, however, allowed to step out together and sit upon their little stools under the roses, or play quietly. In winter all this pleasure came to an end, for the windows were sometimes quite frozen over. But then they would warm copper pennies on the stove, and hold the warm pennies against the frozen pane; there would be very soon a little round hole through which they could peep, and the soft bright eyes of the little boy and girl would beam through the hole at each window as they looked at each other. Their names were Kay and Gerda. In summer they could be together with one jump from the window, but in winter they had to go up and down the long staircase, and out through the snow before they could meet.

"See there are the white bees swarming," said Kay's old grandmother one day when it was snowing.

"Have they a queen bee?" asked the little boy, for he knew that the real bees had a queen.

"To be sure they have," said the grandmother. "She is flying there where the swarm is thickest. She is the largest of them all, and never remains on the earth, but flies up to the dark clouds. Often at midnight she flies through the streets of the town, and looks in at the windows, then the ice freezes on the panes into wonderful shapes, that look like flowers and castles."

"Yes, I have seen them," said both the children, and they knew it must be true.

"Can the Snow Queen come in here?" asked the little girl.

"Only let her come," said the boy. "I'll set her on the stove and then she'll melt."

Then the grandmother smoothed his hair and told

him some more tales. One evening, when little Kay was at home, half undressed, he climbed on a chair by the window and peeped out through the little hole. A few flakes of snow were falling, and one of them, rather larger than the rest, alighted on the edge of one of the flower boxes. This snowflake grew larger and larger, till at last it became the figure of a woman, dressed in garments of white gauze, which looked like millions of starry snowflakes linked together. She was fair and beautiful, but made of ice—shining and glittering ice. Still she was alive and her eyes sparkled like bright stars, but there was neither peace nor rest in their glance. She nodded toward the window and waved her hand. The little boy was frightened and sprang from the chair; at the same moment it seemed as if a large bird flew by the window. On the following day there was a clear frost, and very soon came the spring. The sun shone, the young green leaves burst forth, the swallows built their nests, windows were opened, and the children sat once more in the garden on the roof, high above all the other rooms. How beautiful the roses blossomed this summer. The little girl had learnt a hymn in which roses were spoken of, and then she thought of their own roses, and she sang the hymn to the little boy, and he sang, too:

"Roses bloom and cease to be,

But we shall the Christ-child see."

Then the little ones held each other by the hand, and kissed the roses, and looked at the bright sunshine, and spoke to it as if the Christ-child were there. Those were splendid summer days. How beautiful and fresh it was out among the rosebushes, which seemed as if they would never leave off blooming. One day Kay and Gerda sat looking at a book full of pictures of animals and birds, and then just as the clock in the church tower struck twelve, Kay said, "Oh, something has struck my heart!" and soon after, "There is something in my eye."

The little girl put her arm around his neck, and looked into his eye, but she could see nothing.

"I think it is gone," he said. But it was not gone; it was one of those bits of the looking glass—that magic mirror, of which we have spoken—the ugly glass that made everything great and good appear small and ugly, while all that was wicked and bad became more visible, and every little fault could be plainly seen. Poor little Kay had also received a small grain in his heart, which very quickly turned to a lump of ice. He felt no more pain, but the glass was there still. "Why do you cry?" said he at last. "It makes you look ugly. There is nothing the matter with me now. Oh, see!" he cried suddenly. "That rose is worm-eaten, and this one is quite crooked. After all, they are ugly roses, just like the box in which they stand,"

and then he kicked the boxes with his foot, and pulled off the two roses.

"Kay, what are you doing?" cried the little girl, and then, when he saw how frightened she was, he tore off another rose, and jumped through his own window away from little Gerda.

When she afterward brought out the picture book, he said, "It was only fit for babies in long clothes," and when grandmother told any stories, he would interrupt her with "but"; or, when he could manage it, he would get behind her chair, put on a pair of spectacles, and imitate her very cleverly, to make people laugh. By and by he began to mimic the speech and gait of people in the street. All that was peculiar or disagreeable in a person he would imitate directly, and people said, "That boy will be very clever, he has a remarkable genius." But it was the piece of glass in his eye, and the coldness in his heart, that made him act like this. He would even tease little Gerda, who loved him with all her heart. His games, too, were quite different; they were not so childish. One winter's day, when it snowed, he brought out a special lens, then he held out the tail of his blue coat, and let the snowflakes fall upon it. "Look in this glass, Gerda," said he; and she saw how every flake of snow was magnified, and looked like a beautiful flower or a glittering star. "Is it not clever?" said Kay. "And much more interesting than looking at real flowers. There is not a single fault in it, and the snowflakes are quite perfect till they begin to melt."

Soon after, Kay made his appearance in large thick gloves, and with his sled at his back. He called upstairs to Gerda, "I've got to leave to go into the great square, where the other boys play and ride." And away he went.

In the great square, the boldest among the boys would often tie their sleds to the country people's carts, and go with them a good way. This was capital. But while they were all amusing themselves, and Kay with them, a great sled came by. It was painted white, and in it sat someone wrapped in a rough white fur, and wearing a white cap. The sled drove twice around the square, and Kay fastened his own little sled to it, so that when it went away, he followed with it. It went faster and faster right through the next street, and then the person who drove turned around and nodded pleasantly to Kay, just as if they were acquainted with each other, but whenever Kay wished to loosen his little sled the driver nodded again, so Kay sat still, and they drove out through the town gate. Then the snow began to fall so heavily that the little boy could not see a hand's breadth before him, but still they drove on; then he suddenly loosened the cord so that the large sled might go on without him, but it was of no use; his little carriage held fast, and away they went like the wind. Then he called out loudly, but nobody heard him, while the snow beat upon him, and the sled flew onward. Every now and then it gave a jump as if it were going over hedges and ditches. The boy was frightened and tried to say a prayer, but he could remember nothing but the multiplication table.

The snowflakes became larger and larger, till they appeared like great white chickens. All at once they sprang on one side, the great sled stopped, and the person who had driven it rose up. The fur and the cap, which were made entirely of snow, fell off, and he saw a lady, tall and white, it was the Snow Queen.

"We have driven well," said she, "but why do you tremble? Here, creep into my warm fur." Then she seated him beside her in the sled, and as she wrapped the fur around him he felt as if he were sinking into a snow drift.

"Are you still cold?" she asked, as she kissed him on the forehead. The kiss was colder than ice; it went quite through to his heart, which was already almost a lump of ice; he felt as if he were going to die, but only for a moment; he soon seemed quite well again, and did not notice the cold around him.

"My sled! don't forget my sled," was his first thought, and then he looked and saw that it was bound fast to one of the white chickens, which flew behind him with the sled at its back. The Snow Queen kissed little Kay again, and by this time he had forgotten little Gerda, his grandmother, and all at home.

"Now you must have no more kisses," she said, "or I should kiss you to death."

Kay looked at her, and saw that she was so beautiful; he could not imagine a more lovely and intelligent face;

she did not now seem to be made of ice, as when he had seen her through his window, and she had nodded to him. In his eyes she was perfect, and she did not feel at all afraid. He told her he could do mental arithmetic, as far as fractions, and that he knew the number of square miles and the number of inhabitants in the country. And she always smiled so that he thought he did not know enough yet, and she looked around the vast expanse as she flew higher and higher with him upon a black cloud, while the storm blew and howled as if it were singing old songs. They flew over woods and lakes, over sea and land; below them roared the wild wind; the wolves howled and the snow crackled; over them flew the black screaming crows, and above all shone the moon, clear and bright—and so Kay passed through the long winter's night, and by day he slept at the feet of the Snow Queen.

Third Story

The Flower Garden of the Woman
Who Could Conjure

But how fared little Gerda during Kay's absence? What had become of him, no one knew, nor could anyone give the slightest information, except the boys, who said that he had tied his sled to another very large one, which had driven through the street and out at the town gate. Nobody knew where it went; many tears were shed for him, and little Gerda wept bitterly for a long time. She said she knew he must be dead; that he was drowned in the river that flowed close by the school. Oh, indeed those long winter days were very dreary. But at last spring came, with warm sunshine. "Kay is dead and gone," said little Gerda.

"I don't believe it," said the sunshine.

"He is dead and gone," she said to the sparrows.

"We don't believe it," they replied; and at last little Gerda began to doubt it herself. "I will put on my new red shoes," she said one morning, "those that Kay has never seen, and then I will go down to the river and ask for him." It was quite early when she kissed her old grandmother, who was still asleep; then she put on her red shoes, and went quite alone out of the town gates toward the river. "Is it true that you have taken my little playmate away from me?" said she to the river. "I will give you my red shoes if you will give him back to me." And it seemed as if the waves nodded to her in a strange manner. Then she took off her red shoes, which she liked better than anything else, and threw them both into the river, but they fell near the bank, and the little waves carried them back to the land, just as if the river would not take from her what she loved best, because they could not give her back little Kay. But she thought the shoes had not been thrown out far enough. Then she crept into a boat that lay among the reeds, and threw the shoes again from the farther end of the boat into the water, but it was not fastened. And her movement sent it gliding away from the land. When she saw this she hastened to reach the end of the boat, but before she could so it was more than a yard from the bank, and drifting away faster than ever. Then little Gerda was very much frightened, and began to cry, but no one heard her except the sparrows, and they could not carry her to land, but they flew along by the shore, and sang, as if to comfort her, "Here we are! Here we are!" The boat floated with the stream; little Gerda sat quite still with only her stockings on her feet; the red shoes floated after her, but she could not reach them because the boat kept so much in advance. The banks on each side of the river were very pretty. There were beautiful flowers, old trees, sloping fields, in which cows and sheep were grazing, but not a man to be seen. *Perhaps the river will carry me to little Kay*, thought Gerda, and then she became more cheerful, and raised her head, and looked at the beautiful green banks; and so the boat sailed on for hours. At length she came to a large cherry orchard, in which stood a small red house with strange red and blue windows. It had also a thatched roof, and outside were two wooden soldiers that presented arms to her as she sailed past. Gerda called out to them, for she thought they were alive, but of course they did not answer; and as the boat drifted nearer to the shore, she saw what they really were. Then Gerda called still louder, and there came a very old woman out of the house, leaning on a crutch. She wore a large hat to shade her from the sun, and on it were painted all sorts of pretty flowers. "You poor little child," said the old woman, "how did you manage to come all this distance into the wide world on such a rapid rolling stream?" And then the old woman walked in the water, seized the boat with her crutch, drew it to land, and lifted Gerda out. And Gerda was glad to feel herself on dry ground, although she was rather afraid of the strange old woman. "Come and tell me who you are," said she, "and how came you here."

Then Gerda told her everything, while the old woman shook her head, and said, "Hem-hem"; and when she had finished, Gerda asked if she had not seen little Kay, and the old woman told her he had not passed by that way, but he very likely would come. So she told Gerda not to be sorrowful, but to taste the cherries and look at the flowers; they were better than any picture book, for each of them could tell a story. Then she took Gerda by the hand and led her into the little house, and the old woman closed the door. The windows were very high, and as the panes were red, blue, and yellow, the daylight shone through them in all sorts of singular colors. On the table stood beautiful cherries, and Gerda had permission to eat as many as she could. While she was eating them the old woman combed out her long flaxen ringlets with a golden comb, and the glossy curls hung down on each side of the little round pleasant face, which looked fresh and blooming as a rose. "I have long been wishing for a dear little maiden like you," said the old woman, "and now you must stay with me and see how happily we shall live together." And while the old woman went on combing her hair, Gerda thought less and less about her adopted brother Kay, for the old woman could conjure, although she was not a wicked witch; she conjured only a little for her own amusement, and now, because she wanted to keep Gerda. Therefore she went into the garden, and stretched out her crutch toward all the rose trees, beautiful though they were; and they immediately sank into the dark earth, so that no one could tell where they had once stood. The old woman was afraid that if little Gerda saw roses she would think of those at home, and then remember little Kay and run away. Then she took Gerda into the flower garden. How fragrant and beautiful it was! Every flower that could be thought of for every season of the year was here in full bloom; no picture book could have more beautiful colors. Gerda jumped for joy, and played till the sun went down behind the tall cherry trees; then she slept in an elegant bed with red silk pillows embroidered with colored violets; and then she dreamed as pleasantly as a queen on her wedding day. The next day, and for many days after, Gerda played with the flowers in the warm sunshine. She knew every flower, and yet, although there were so many of them, it seemed as if one were missing, but which it was she could not tell. One day, however, as she sat looking at the old woman's hat with the painted flowers on it, she saw that the prettiest of them all was a rose. The old woman had forgotten to take it from her hat when she made all the roses sink into the earth. But it is difficult to keep the thoughts together in everything; one little mistake upsets all our arrangements.

"What, are there no roses here?" cried Gerda; and she ran out into the garden, and examined all the beds, and searched and searched. There was not one to be found. Then she sat down and wept, and her tears fell just on the place where one of the rose trees had sunk down. The warm tears moistened the earth, and the rose tree sprouted up at once, as blooming as when it had sunk; and Gerda embraced it and kissed the roses, and thought of the beautiful roses at home, and, with them, of little Kay.

"Oh, how I have been detained!" said the little maiden. "I wanted to seek for little Kay. Do you know where he is?" she asked the roses. "Do you think he is dead?"

And the roses answered, "No, he is not dead. We have

been in the ground where all the dead lie; but Kay is not there."

"Thank you," said little Gerda, and then she went to the other flowers, and looked into their little cups, and asked, "Do you know where little Kay is?" But each flower, as it stood in the sunshine, dreamed only of its own little fairy tale of history. Not one knew anything of Kay. Gerda heard many stories from the flowers, as she asked them one after another about him.

And what said the Tiger Lily? "Hark, do you hear the drum?—'turn, turn,'—there are only two notes, always, 'turn, turn.' Listen to the women's song of mourning! Hear the cry of the priest! In her long red robe stands the widow by the funeral pile. The flames rise around her as she places herself on the dead body of her husband, but the woman is thinking of the living one in that circle; of him, her son, who lighted those flames. Those shining eyes trouble her heart more painfully than the flames that will soon consume her body to ashes. Can the fire of the heart be extinguished in the flames of the funeral pile?"

"I don't understand that at all," said little Gerda.

"That is my story," said the Tiger Lily.

What says the shrub? "Near yonder narrow road stands an old knight's castle; thick ivy creeps over the old ruined walls, leaf over leaf, even to the balcony, in which stands a beautiful maiden. She bends over the balustrades and looks up the road. No rose on its stem is fresher than she; no apple blossom, wafted by the wind, floats more lightly than she moves. Her rich silk rustles as she bends over and exclaims, "Will he not come?""

"Is it Kay you mean?" asked Gerda.

"I am only speaking of a story of my dream," replied the shrub.

What said the little snowdrop? "Between two trees a

rope is hanging; there is a piece of board upon it; it is a swing. Two pretty little girls, in dresses white as snow, and with long green ribbons fluttering from their hats, are sitting upon it swinging. Their brother, who is taller than they are, stands on the swing; he has one arm around the rope, to steady himself; in one hand he holds a little bowl, and in the other a clay pipe; he is blowing bubbles. As the swing goes on, the bubbles fly upward, reflecting the most beautiful varying colors. The last still hangs from the bowl of the pipe, and sways in the wind. On goes the swing; and then a little black dog comes running up. He is almost as light as the bubble, and he raises himself on his hind legs and wants to be taken onto the swing; but it does not stop, and the dog falls; then he barks and gets angry. The children stoop toward him, and the bubble bursts. A swinging plank, a light sparkling foam picture—that is my story."

"It may be all very pretty what you are telling me," said

little Gerda, "but you speak so mournfully, and you do not mention little Kay at all."

What do the Hyacinths say? "There were three beautiful sisters, fair and delicate. The dress of one was red, of the second blue, and of the third pure white. Hand-in-hand they danced in the bright moonlight by the calm lake; but they were human beings, not fairy elves. The sweet fragrance attracted them, and they disappeared in the wood; here the fragrance became stronger. Three coffins, in which lay the three beautiful maidens, glided from the thickest part of the forest across the lake. The fireflies flew lightly over them, like little floating torches. Do the dancing maidens sleep, or are they dead? The scent of the flower says that they are corpses. The evening bell tolls their knell."

"You make me quite sorrowful," said little Gerda. "Your perfume is so strong, you make me think of the dead maidens. Ah! Is little Kay really dead, then? The roses have been in the earth, and they say no."

"Cling, clang," tolled the hyacinth bells. "We are not tolling for little Kay; we do not know him. We sing our song, the only one we know."

Then Gerda went to the buttercups that were glittering among the bright green leaves.

"You are little bright suns," said Gerda; "tell me if you know where I can find my playfellow."

And the buttercups sparkled joyfully, and looked again at Gerda. What song could the buttercups sing? It was not about Kay.

"The bright warm sun shone on a little court, on the first warm day of spring. His bright beams rested on the white walls of the neighboring house; and close by bloomed the first yellow flower of the season, glittering like gold in the sun's warm rays. An old woman sat in her armchair at the house door, and her granddaughter, a poor and pretty servant maid, came to see her for a short visit. When she kissed her grandmother there was gold everywhere: the gold of the heart in that holy kiss; it was a golden morning; there was gold in the beaming sunlight, gold in the leaves of the lowly flower, and on the lips of the maiden. There, that is my story," said the buttercup.

"My poor old grandmother!" sighed Gerda. "She is longing to see me, and grieving for me as she did for little Kay; but I shall soon go home now, and take little Kay with me. It is no use asking the flowers; they know only their own songs, and can give me no information."

And then she tucked up her little dress, that she might run faster, but the narcissus caught her by the leg as she was jumping over it; so she stopped and looked at the tall yellow flower, and said, "Perhaps you may know something."

Then she stooped down quite close to the flower, and listened; and what did he say?

"I can see myself, I can see myself," said the narcissus. "Oh, how sweet is my perfume! Up in a little room with a bow window, stands a little dancing girl, half undressed; she stands sometimes on one leg, and sometimes on both, and looks as if she would tread the whole world under her feet. She is nothing but a delusion. She is pouring water out of a teapot on a piece of stuff, which she holds in her hand; it is her bodice. "Cleanliness is a good thing," she says. Her white dress hangs on a peg; it has also been washed in the teapot, and dried on the roof. She puts it on, and ties a saffron-colored handkerchief around her neck, which makes the dress look whiter. See how she stretches out her legs, as if she were showing off on a stem. I can see myself, I can see myself."

"What do I care for all that," said Gerda. "You need not tell me such stuff." And then she ran to the other end of the garden. The door was fastened, but she pressed against the rusty latch, and it gave way. The door sprang open, and little Gerda ran out with bare feet into the wide world. She looked back three times, but no one seemed to be following her. At last she could run no longer, so she sat down to rest on a great stone, and when she looked around she saw that the summer was over, and autumn very far advanced. She had known nothing of this in the beautiful garden, where the sun shone and the flowers grew all the year around.

"Oh, how I have wasted my time," said little Gerda. "It is autumn. I must not rest any longer," and she rose up to go on. But her little feet were wounded and sore, and everything around her looked so cold and bleak. The long willow leaves were quite yellow. The dewdrops fell like water, leaf after leaf dropped from the trees, the blackthorn alone still bore fruit, but the blackthorns were sour, and set the teeth on edge. Oh, how dark and weary the whole world appeared!

Fourth Story

The Prince and Princess

Gerda was obliged to rest again, and just opposite the place where she sat, she saw a great crow come hopping across the snow toward her. He stood looking at her for some time, and then he wagged his head and said, "Caw, caw; good day, good day." He pronounced the words as plainly as he could, because he meant to be kind to the little girl; and then he asked her where she was going all alone in the wide world.

The word alone Gerda understood very well, and knew how much it expressed. So then she told the crow the whole story of her life and adventures, and asked him if he had seen little Kay.

The crow nodded his head very gravely, and said, "Perhaps I have—it may be."

"No! Do you think you have?" cried little Gerda, and she kissed the crow, and hugged him almost to death with joy.

"Gently, gently," said the crow. "I believe I know. I think it may be little Kay; but he has certainly forgotten you by this time for the princess."

"Does he live with a princess?" asked Gerda.

"Yes, listen," replied the crow, "but it is so difficult to speak your language. If you understand the crows' language, then I can explain it better. Do you?"

"No, I have never learnt it," said Gerda, "but my

grandmother understands it, and used to speak it to me. I wish I had learnt it."

"It does not matter," answered the crow. "I will explain as well as I can, although it will be very badly done," and he told her what he had heard. "In this kingdom where we now are," said he, "there lives a princess, who is so wonderfully clever that she has read all the newspapers in the world, and forgotten them, too, although she is so clever. A short time ago, as she was sitting on her throne, which people say is not such an agreeable seat as is often supposed, she began to sing a song which commences in these words: "Why should I not be married?"

"Why not indeed?" said she, and so she determined to marry if she could find a husband who knew what to say when he was spoken to, and not one who could only look grand, for that was so tiresome. Then she assembled all her court ladies together at the beat of the drum, and when they heard of her intentions they were very much pleased. 'We are so glad to hear it,' said they, 'we were talking about it ourselves the other day.' You may believe that every word I tell you is true," said the crow, "for I have a tame sweetheart who goes freely about the palace, and she told me all this."

Of course his sweetheart was a crow, for "birds of a feather flock together," and one crow always chooses another crow.

"Newspapers were published immediately, with a border of hearts, and the initials of the princess among them. They gave notice that every young man who was handsome was free to visit the castle and speak with the princess; and those who could reply loud enough to be heard when spoken to were to make themselves quite at home at the palace; but the one who spoke best would be chosen as a husband for the princess. Yes, yes, you may believe me, it is all as true as I sit here," said the crow.

"The people came in crowds. There was a great deal of crushing and running about, but no one succeeded either on the first or second day. They could all speak very well while they were outside in the streets, but when they entered the palace gates, and saw the guards in silver uniforms, and the footmen in their golden livery on the staircase, and the great halls lighted up, they became quite confused. And when they stood before the throne on which the princess sat, they could do nothing but repeat the last words she had said; and she had no particular wish to hear her own words over again. It was just as if they had all taken something to make them sleepy while they were in the palace, for they did not recover themselves nor speak till they got back again into the street. There was quite a long line of them reaching from the town gate to the palace. I went myself to see them," said the crow. "They were hungry and thirsty, for at the palace they did not get even a glass of water. Some of the wisest had taken a few slices of bread and butter with them, but they did not share it with their neighbors; they thought if they went in to the princess looking hungry, there would be a better chance for themselves."

"But Kay! Tell me about little Kay!" said Gerda. "Was he among the crowd?"

"Stop a bit, we are just coming to him. It was on the third day, there came marching cheerfully along to the palace a little personage, without horses or carriage, his eyes sparkling like yours; he had beautiful long hair, but his clothes were very poor."

"That was Kay!" said Gerda joyfully. "Oh, then I have found him," and she clapped her hands.

"He had a little knapsack on his back," added the crow.

"No, it must have been his sledge," said Gerda, "for he went away with it."

"It may have been so," said the crow. "I did not look at it very closely. But I know from my tame sweetheart that he passed through the palace gates, saw the guards in their silver uniforms, and the servants in their liveries of gold on the stairs, but he was not in the least embarrassed. 'It must be very tiresome to stand on the stairs,' he said. 'I prefer to go in.' The rooms were blazing with light. Councilors and ambassadors walked about with bare feet, carrying golden vessels; it was enough to make anyone feel serious. His boots creaked loudly as he walked, and yet he was not at all uneasy."

"It must be Kay," said Gerda. "I know he had new boots on; I have heard them creak in Grandmother's room."

"They really did creak," said the crow, "yet he went boldly up to the princess herself, who was sitting on a pearl as large as a spinning wheel, and all the ladies of the court were present with their maids, and all the cavaliers with their servants; and each of the maids had another maid to wait upon her, and the cavaliers' servants had their own servants, as well as a page each. They all stood in circles around the princess, and the nearer they stood to the door, the prouder they looked. The servants' pages, who always wore slippers, could hardly be looked at, they held themselves up so proudly by the door."

"It must be quite awful," said little Gerda, "but did Kay win the princess?"

"If I had not been a crow," said he, "I would have married her myself, although I am engaged. He spoke just as well as I do, when I speak the crows' language, so I heard from my tame sweetheart. He was quite free and agreeable and said he had not come to woo the princess, but to hear her wisdom; and he was as pleased with her as she was with him."

"Oh, certainly that was Kay," said Gerda. "He was so clever; he could work mental arithmetic and fractions. Oh, will you take me to the palace?"

"It is very easy to ask that," replied the crow, "but how are we to manage it? However, I will speak about it to my tame sweetheart, and ask her advice; for I must tell you it will be very difficult to gain permission for a little girl like you to enter the palace."

"Oh, yes; but I shall gain permission easily," said Gerda, "for when Kay hears that I am here, he will come out and fetch me in immediately."

"Wait for me here by the palings," said the crow, wagging his head as he flew away.

It was late in the evening before the crow returned. "Caw, caw," he said, "she sends you greeting, and here is a little roll which she took from the kitchen for you; there is plenty of bread there, and she thinks you must be hungry. It is not possible for you to enter the palace by the front entrance. The guards in silver uniform and the servants in gold livery would not allow it. But do not cry, we will manage to get you in; my sweetheart knows a little back staircase that leads to the sleeping apartments, and she knows where to find the key."

Then they went into the garden through the great avenue, where the leaves were falling one after another, and they could see the light in the palace being put out in the same manner. And the crow led little Gerda to the back door, which stood ajar. Oh! How little Gerda's heart beat with anxiety and longing; it was just as if she were going to do something wrong, and yet she only wanted to know where little Kay was. "It must be he," she thought, "with those clear eyes, and that long hair." She could fancy she saw him smiling at her, as he used to at home, when they sat among the roses. He would certainly be glad to see her, and to hear what a long distance she had come for his sake, and to know how sorry they had been at home because he did not come back. Oh what joy and yet fear she felt! They were now on the stairs, and in a small closet at the top a lamp was burning. In the middle of the floor stood the tame crow, turning her head from side to side, and gazing at Gerda, who curtsyed as her grandmother had taught her to do.

"My betrothed has spoken so very highly of you, my little lady," said the tame crow. "Your life history, Vita, as it may be called, is very touching. If you will take the lamp I will walk before you. We will go straight along this way, then we shall meet no one."

"It seems to me as if somebody were behind us," said Gerda, as something rushed by her like a shadow on the wall, and then horses with flying manes and thin legs, hunters, ladies and gentlemen on horseback, glided by her, like shadows on the wall.

"They are only dreams," said the crow, "they are coming to fetch the thoughts of the great people out hunting."

"All the better, for we shall be able to look at them in

their beds more safely. I hope that when you rise to honor and favor, you will show a grateful heart."

"You may be quite sure of that," said the crow from the forest.

They now came into the first hall, the walls of which were hung with rose-colored satin embroidered with artificial flowers. Here the dreams again flitted by them but so quickly that Gerda could not distinguish the royal persons. Each hall appeared more splendid than the last; it was enough to bewilder anyone. At length they reached a bedroom. The ceiling was like a great palm tree, with glass leaves of the most costly crystal, and over the center of the floor two beds, each resembling a lily, hung from a stem of gold. One, in which the princess lay, was white, the other was red; and in this Gerda had to seek for little Kay. She pushed one of the red leaves aside, and saw a little brown neck. Oh, that must be Kay! She called his name out quite loud, and held the lamp over him. The dreams rushed back into the room on horseback. He woke, and turned his head around; it was not little Kay! The prince was only like him in the neck; still he was young and pretty. Then the princess peeped out of her white-lily bed, and asked what was the matter. Then little Gerda wept and told her story, and all that the crows had done to help her.

"You poor child," said the prince and princess; then they praised the crows, and said they were not angry for what they had done, but that it must not happen again, and this time they should be rewarded.

"Would you like to have your freedom?" asked the princess. "Or would you prefer to be raised to the position of court crows, with all that is left in the kitchen for yourselves?"

Then both the crows bowed, and begged to have a fixed appointment, for they thought of their old age, and said it would be so comfortable to feel that they had provision for their old days, as they called it. And then the prince got out of his bed, and gave it up to Gerda—he could do no more; and she lay down. She folded her little hands, and thought, *How good everyone is to me, men and animals, too.* Then she closed her eyes and fell into a sweet sleep. All the dreams came flying back again to her, and they looked like angels, and one of them drew a little sledge, on which sat Kay, and nodded to her. But all this was only a dream, and vanished as soon as she awoke.

The following day she was dressed from head to foot in silk and velvet, and they invited her to stay at the palace for a few days, and enjoy herself, but she only begged for a pair of boots, and a little carriage, and a horse to draw it, so that she might go into the wide world to seek for Kay. And she obtained, not only boots, but also a muff, and she was neatly dressed; and when she was ready to go, there, at the door, she found a coach made of pure gold, with the coat of arms of the prince and princess shining upon it like a star, and the coachman, footman, and outriders all wearing golden crowns on their heads. The prince and princess themselves helped her into the coach, and wished her success. The forest crow, who was now married, accompanied her for the first three miles; he sat by Gerda's side, as he could not bear riding backward. The tame crow stood in the doorway flapping her wings. She could not go with them, because she had been suffering from headache ever since the new appointment, no doubt from eating too much. The coach was well stored with sweet cakes, and under the seat were fruit and gingerbread nuts. "Farewell, farewell," cried the prince and princess, and little Gerda wept, and the crow wept; and then, after a few miles, the crow also said, "Farewell," and this was the saddest parting. However, he flew to a tree, and stood flapping his black wings as long as he could see the coach, which glittered in the bright sunshine.

Fifth Story

Little Robber-Girl

The coach drove on through a thick forest, where it lighted up the way like a torch, and dazzled the eyes of some robbers, who could not bear to let it pass them unexamined.

"It is gold! It is gold!" cried they, rushing forward and seizing the horses. Then they struck the little jockeys, the coachman, and the footman dead, and pulled little Gerda out of the carriage.

"She is fat and pretty, and she has been fed with the kernels of nuts," said the old robber-woman, who had a long beard and eyebrows that hung over her eyes. "She is as good as a little lamb; how nice she will taste!" and as she said this, she drew forth a shining knife that glittered horribly. "Oh!" screamed the old woman the same moment; for her own daughter, who held her back, had bitten her in the ear. She was a wild and naughty girl, and the mother called her an ugly thing, and had not time to kill Gerda.

"She shall play with me," said the little robber-girl. "She shall give me her muff and her pretty dress, and sleep with me in my bed." And then she bit her mother again, and made her spring in the air and jump about; and all the robbers laughed and said, "See how she is dancing with her young cub."

"I will have a ride in the coach," said the little robber-girl; and she would have her own way, for she was so self-willed and obstinate.

She and Gerda seated themselves in the coach, and drove away, over stumps and stones, into the depths of the forest. The little robber-girl was about the same size as Gerda, but stronger; she had broader shoulders and a darker skin; her eyes were quite black, and she had a mournful look. She clasped little Gerda around the waist, and said, "They shall not kill you as long as you don't make us vexed with you. I suppose you are a princess."

"No," said Gerda, and then she told her all her history, and how fond she was of little Kay.

The robber-girl looked earnestly at her, nodded her head slightly, and said, "They shan't kill you, even if I do get angry with you; for I will do it myself." And then she wiped Gerda's eyes, and stuck her own hands in the beautiful muff, which was so soft and warm.

The coach stopped in the courtyard of a robber's castle, the walls of which were cracked from top to bottom. Ravens and crows flew in and out of the holes and crevices, while great bulldogs, either of which looked as if it could swallow a man, were jumping about; but they were not allowed to bark. In the large and smoky hall a bright fire was burning on the stone floor. There was no chimney; so the smoke went up to the ceiling and found a way out for itself. Soup was boiling in a large cauldron, and hares and rabbits were roasting on the spit.

"You shall sleep with me and all my little animals tonight," said the robber-girl, after they had had something to eat and drink. So she took Gerda to a corner of the hall, where some straw and carpets were laid down. Above them, on laths and perches, were more than a hundred pigeons, who all seemed to be asleep, although they moved slightly when the two little girls came near them. "These all belong to me," said the robber-girl; and she seized the nearest to her, held it by the feet, and shook it till it flapped its wings. "Kiss it," cried she, flapping it in Gerda's face. "There sit the wood pigeons," continued she, pointing to a number of laths and a cage, which had been fixed into the walls, near one of the openings. "Both rascals would fly away directly, if they were not closely locked up. And here is my old sweetheart 'Ba'"; and she dragged out a reindeer by the horn; he wore a bright copper ring around his neck and was tied up. "We are obliged to hold him tight, too, or else he would run away from us also. I tickle his neck every evening with my sharp knife, which frightens him very much." And then the robber-girl drew a long knife from a chink in the wall, and let it slide gently over the reindeer's neck. The poor animal began to kick, and the little robber-girl laughed, and pulled down Gerda into bed with her.

"Will you have that knife with you while you are asleep?" asked Gerda, looking at it in great fright.

"I always sleep with the knife by me," said the robber-girl. "No one knows what may happen. But now tell me again all about little Kay, and why you went out into the world."

Then Gerda repeated her story over again, while the wood pigeons in the cage over her cooed, and the other pigeons slept. The little robber-girl put one arm across Gerda's neck, and held the knife in the other, and was soon fast asleep and snoring. But Gerda could not close her eyes at all; she knew not whether she was to live or die. The robbers sat around the fire, singing and drinking, and the old woman stumbled about. It was a terrible sight for a little girl to witness.

Then the wood pigeons said, "Coo, coo; we have seen little Kay. A white fowl carried his sledge, and he sat in the carriage of the Snow Queen, which drove through the wood while we were lying in our nest. She blew upon us, and all the young ones died except us two. Coo, coo."

"What are you saying up there?" cried Gerda. "Where was the Snow Queen going? Do you know anything about it?"

"She was most likely traveling to Lapland, where there is always snow and ice. Ask the reindeer that is fastened up there with a rope."

"Yes, there is always snow and ice," said the reindeer, "and it is a glorious place; you can leap and run about freely on the sparkling ice plains. The Snow Queen has her summer tent there, but her strong castle is at the North Pole, on an island called Spitzbergen."

"Oh, Kay, little Kay!" sighed Gerda.

"Lie still," said the robber-girl, "or I shall run my knife into your body."

In the morning Gerda told her all that the wood pigeons had said; and the little robber-girl looked quite serious, and nodded her head, and said, "That is all talk, that is all talk. Do you know where Lapland is?" she asked the reindeer.

"Who should know better than I do?" said the animal, while his eyes sparkled. "I was born and brought up there, and used to run about the snow-covered plains."

"Now listen," said the robber girl, "all our men are gone away—only mother is here, and here she will stay; but at noon she always drinks out of a great bottle, and afterward sleeps for a little while; and then, I'll do something for you." Then she jumped out of bed, clasped her mother around the neck, and pulled her by the beard, crying, "My own little nanny goat, good morning." Then her mother flicked her nose till it was quite red; yet she did it all for love.

When the mother had drunk out of the bottle, and was gone to sleep, the little robber-maiden went to the reindeer, and said, "I should like very much to tickle your neck a few times more with my knife, for it makes you look so funny; but never mind—I will untie your cord and set you free, so that you may run away to Lapland; but you must make good use of your legs, and carry this little maiden to the castle of the Snow Queen, where her play-fellow is. You have heard what she told me, for she spoke loud enough, and you were listening."

Then the reindeer jumped for joy; and the little robber-girl lifted Gerda on his back, and had the fore-thought to tie her on, and even to give her her own little cushion to sit on.

"Here are your fur boots for you," said she. "For it will be very cold; but I must keep the muff; it is so pretty. However, you shall not be frozen for the want of it; here are my mother's large warm mittens; they will reach up to your elbows. Let me put them on. There, now your hands look just like my mother's."

But Gerda wept for joy.

"I don't like to see you fret," said the little robber-girl. "You ought to look quite happy now; and here are two loaves and a ham, so that you need not starve." These were fastened on the reindeer, and then the little robber maiden opened the door, coaxed in all the great dogs, and then with her sharp knife, cut the string with which the reindeer was fastened, and said, "Now run, but mind you take good care of the little girl." And then Gerda stretched out her hand, with the great mitten on it, toward the little robber-girl, and said, "Farewell," and away flew the reindeer, over stumps and stones, through the great forest, over marshes and plains, as quickly as he could. The wolves howled, and the ravens screamed; while up in the sky quivered red lights like flames of fire. "There are my old northern lights," said the reindeer. "See how they flash." And he ran on day and night still faster and faster, but the loaves and the ham were all eaten by the time they reached Lapland.

Sixth Story

The Lapland Woman and the Finland Woman

They stopped at a little hut; it was very mean-looking; the roof sloped nearly down to the ground, and the door was so low that the family had to creep in on their hands and knees when they went in and out. There was no one at home but an old Lapland woman, who was cooking fish by the light of a train-oil lamp. The reindeer told her all about Gerda's story, after having first told his own, which seemed to him the most important, but Gerda was so pinched with the cold that she could not speak. "Oh, you poor things," said the Lapland woman, "you have a long way to go yet. You must travel more than a hundred miles farther to Finland. The Snow Queen lives there now, and she burns Bengal lights every evening. I will write a few words on a dried stockfish, for I have no paper, and you can take it from me to the Finland woman who lives there; she can give you better information than I can." So when Gerda was warmed, and had taken something to eat and drink, the woman wrote a few words on the dried fish, and told Gerda to take great care of it. Then she tied her again on the reindeer, and he set off.at full speed. Flash, flash, went the beautiful blue northern lights in the air the whole night long. And at length they reached Finland, and knocked at the chimney of the Finland woman's hut, for it had no door above the ground. They crept in, but it was so terribly hot inside that that woman wore scarcely any clothes; she was small and very dirty-looking. She loosened little Gerda's dress, and took off the fur boots and the mittens, or Gerda would have been unable to bear the heat; and then she placed a piece of ice on the reindeer's head, and read what was written on the dried fish. After she had read it three times, she knew it by heart, so she popped the fish into the soup saucepan, as she knew it was good to eat, and she never wasted anything. The reindeer told his own story first, and then little Gerda's, and the Finlander twinkled with her clever eyes, but she said nothing. "You are so clever," said the reindeer. "I know you can tie all the winds of the world with a piece of twine. If a sailor unties one knot, he has a fair wind; when he unties the second, it blows hard; but if the third and fourth are loosened, then comes a storm, which will root up whole forests. Cannot you give this little maiden something that will make her as strong as twelve men, to overcome the Snow Queen?"

"The power of twelve men!" said the Finland woman. "That would be of very little use." But she went to a shelf and took down and unrolled a large skin, on which were inscribed wonderful characters, and she read till the perspiration ran down from her forehead. But the reindeer begged so hard for little Gerda, and Gerda looked at the Finland woman with such beseeching tearful eyes, that her own eyes began to twinkle again; so she drew the reindeer into a corner, and whispered to him while she laid a fresh piece of ice on his head, "Little Kay is really with the Snow Queen, but he finds everything there so much to his taste and his liking that he believes it is the finest place in the world; but this is because he has a piece of broken glass in his heart, and a little piece of glass in his eye. These must be taken out, or he will never be a human being again, and the Snow Queen will retain her power over him."

"But can you not give little Gerda something to help her to conquer this power?"

"I can give her no greater power than she has already," said the woman. "Don't you see how strong that is? How men and animals are obliged to serve her, and how well she has got through the world, barefooted as she is. She cannot receive any power from me greater than she now has, which consists in her own purity and innocence of heart. If she cannot herself obtain access to the Snow Queen, and remove the glass fragments from little Kay, we can do nothing to help her. Two miles from here the Snow Queen's garden begins; you can carry the little girl so far, and set her down by the large bush, which stands in the snow, covered with red berries. Do not stay gossiping, but come back here as quickly as you can." Then the

Finland woman lifted little Gerda upon the reindeer, and he ran away with her as quickly as he could.

"Oh, I have forgotten my boots and my mittens," cried little Gerda, as soon as she felt the cutting cold, but the reindeer dared not stop, so he ran on till he reached the bush with the red berries; here he set Gerda down, and he kissed her, and the great bright tears trickled over the animal's cheeks; then he left her and ran back as fast as he could.

There stood poor Gerda, without shoes, without gloves, in the midst of cold, dreary, ice-bound Finland. She ran forward as quickly as she could, when a whole regiment of snowflakes came around her; they did not, however, fall from the sky, which was quite clear and glittering with the northern lights. The snowflakes ran along the ground, and the nearer they came to her, the larger they appeared. Gerda remembered how large and beautiful they looked through the special lens. But these were really larger, and much more terrible, for they were alive, and were the guards of the Snow Queen, and had the strangest shapes. Some were like great porcupines, others like twisted serpents with their heads stretching out, and some few were like little fat bears with their hair bristled; but all were dazzlingly white, and all were living snowflakes. Then little Gerda repeated the Lord's Prayer, and the cold was so great that she could see her own breath come out of her mouth like steam as she uttered the words. The steam appeared to increase as she continued her prayer, till it took the shape of little angels who grew larger the moment they touched the earth. They all wore helmets on their heads, and carried spears and shields. Their number continued to increase more and more; and by the time Gerda had finished her prayers, a whole legion stood around her. They thrust their spears into the terrible snowflakes, so that they shivered into a hundred pieces, and little Gerda could go forward with courage and safety. The angels stroked her hands and feet, so that she felt the cold less, and she hastened on to the Snow Queen's castle.

But now we must see what Kay is doing. In truth, he thought not of little Gerda, and never supposed she could be standing in the front of the palace.

Seventh Story

Of the Palace of the Snow Queen and What Happened There at Last

The walls of the palace were formed of drifted snow, and the windows and doors of the cutting winds. There were more than a hundred rooms in it, all as if they had been formed with snow blown together. The largest of them extended for several miles; they were all lighted up by the vivid light of the aurora, and they were so large and empty, so icy cold and glittering! There were no amusements here, not even a little bear's ball, when the storm might have been the music, and the bears could have danced on their hind legs and shown their good manners. There were no pleasant games, or even a gossip over the tea table, for the young-lady foxes. Empty, vast, and cold were the halls of the Snow Queen. The flickering flame of the northern lights could be plainly seen, whether they rose high or low in the heavens, from every part of the castle. In the midst of its empty, endless hall of snow was a frozen lake, broken on its surface into a thousand forms; each piece resembled another, from being in itself perfect as a work of art, and in the center of this lake sat the Snow Queen, when she was at home. She called the lake The Mirror of Reason, and said that it was the best, and indeed the only one in the world.

Little Kay was quite blue with cold, indeed almost black, but he did not feel it; for the Snow Queen had kissed away the icy shiverings, and his heart was already a lump of ice. He dragged some sharp, flat pieces of ice to and fro, and placed them together in all kinds of positions, as if he wished to make something out of them; just as we try to form various figures with little tablets of wood. Kay's fingers were very artistic; it was the icy game of reason at which he played, and in his eyes the figures were very remarkable, and of the highest importance; this opinion was owing to the piece of glass still sticking in his eye. He composed many complete figures, forming different words, but there was one word he never could manage to form, although he wished it very much. It was the word *eternity*. The Snow Queen had said to him,

"When you can find out this, you shall be your own master, and I will give you the whole world and a new pair of skates." But he could not accomplish it.

"Now I must hasten away to warmer countries," said the Snow Queen. "I will go and look into the black craters of the tops of the burning mountains, Etna and Vesuvius, as they are called—I shall make them look white, which will be good for them, and for the lemons and the grapes." And away flew the Snow Queen, leaving little Kay quite alone in the great hall, which was so many miles in length; so he sat and looked at his pieces of ice, and was thinking so deeply and sat so still that anyone might have supposed he was frozen.

Just at this moment it happened that little Gerda came through the great door of the castle. Cutting winds were raging around her, but she offered up a prayer and the winds sank down as if they were going to sleep; and she went on till she came to the large empty hall, and caught sight of Kay; she knew him directly; she flew to him and threw her arms around his neck, and held him fast, while she exclaimed, "Kay, dear little Kay, I have found you at last."

But he sat quite still, stiff and cold.

Then little Gerda wept hot tears, which fell on his breast, and penetrated into his heart, and thawed the lump of ice, and washed away the little piece of glass that had stuck there. Then he looked at her, and she sang—

"Roses bloom and cease to be,

But we shall the Christ-child see."

Then Kay burst into tears, and he wept so that the splinter of glass swam out of his eye. Then he recognized Gerda, and said, joyfully, "Gerda, dear little Gerda, where have you been all this time, and where have I been?" And he looked all around him, and said, "How cold it is, and how large and empty it all looks," and he clung to Gerda, and she laughed and wept for joy. It was so pleasing to see them that the pieces of ice even danced about; and when they were tired and went to lie down, they formed themselves into the letters of the word that the Snow Queen had said he must find out before he could be his own master, and have the whole world and a pair of new skates. Then Gerda kissed his cheeks, and they became blooming; and she kissed his eyes, and they shone like her own; she kissed his hands and his feet, and then he became quite healthy and cheerful. The Snow Queen might come home now when she pleased, for there stood his certainty of freedom, in the word she wanted, written in shining letters of ice.

Then they took each other by the hand, and went forth from the great palace of ice. They spoke of the grandmother, and of the roses on the roof, and as they went on the winds were at rest, and the sun burst forth. When they arrived at the bush with red berries, there stood the reindeer waiting for them, and he had brought another young reindeer with him, whose udders were full, and the children drank her warm milk and kissed her on the mouth. Then they carried Kay and Gerda first to the Finland woman, where they warmed themselves thoroughly in the hot room, and she gave them directions about their journey home. Next they went to the Lapland woman, who had made some new clothes for them, and put their sleighs in order. Both the reindeer ran by their side, and followed them as far as the boundaries of the country, where the first green leaves were budding. And here they took leave of the two reindeer and the Lapland woman, and all said, "Farewell." Then the birds began to twitter, and the forest, too, was full of green young leaves; and out of it came a beautiful horse, which Gerda remembered, for it was one which had drawn the golden coach. A young girl was riding upon it, with a shining red cap on her head and pistols in her belt. It was the little robber-maiden, who had got tired of staying at home; she was going first to the north, and if that did not suit her, she meant to try some other part of the world. She knew Gerda directly, and Gerda remembered her: It was a joyful meeting.

"You are a fine fellow to go gadding about in this way," said she to little Kay. "I should like to know whether you deserve that anyone should go to the end of the world to find you."

But Gerda patted her cheeks and asked after the prince and princess.

"They are gone to foreign countries," said the robber-girl.

"And the crow?" asked Gerda.

"Oh, the crow is dead," she replied. "His tame sweetheart is now a widow and wears a bit of black worsted around her leg. She mourns very pitifully, but it is all stuff. But now tell me how you managed to get him back."

Then Gerda and Kay told her all about it.

"Snip, snap, snare! It's all right at last," said the robber-girl.

Then she took both their hands and promised that if ever she should pass through the town, she would call and pay them a visit. And then she rode away into the wide world. But Gerda and Kay went hand in hand toward home; and as they advanced, spring appeared more lovely with its green verdure and its beautiful flowers. Very soon they recognized the large town where they lived, and the tall steeples of the churches, in which the sweet bells were ringing a merry peal as they entered it, and found their way to their grandmother's door. They went upstairs into the little room, where all looked just as it used to do. The old clock was going *tick, tick*, and the hands pointed to the time of day, but as they passed through the door into the room they perceived that they were both grown up, and become a man and woman.

The roses out on the roof were in full bloom, and peeped in at the window; and there stood the little chairs, on which they had sat when children; and Kay and Gerda seated themselves each on their own chair, and held each other by the hand, while the cold empty grandeur of the Snow Queen's palace vanished from their memories like a painful dream. The grandmother sat in God's bright sunshine, and she read aloud from the Bible, "Except ye become as little children, ye shall in no wise enter into the kingdom of God." And Kay and Gerda looked into each other's eyes, and all at once understood the words of the old song,

"Roses bloom and cease to be,

But we shall the Christ-child see."

And they both sat there, grown up, yet children at heart; and it was summer—warm, beautiful summer.

The Ugly Duckling

It was lovely summer weather in the country, and the golden corn, the green oats, and the haystacks piled up in the meadows looked beautiful. The stork walking about on his long red legs chattered in the Egyptian language, which he had learnt from his mother. The cornfields and meadows were surrounded by large forests, in the midst of which were deep pools. It was, indeed, delightful to walk about in the country. In a sunny spot stood a pleasant old farmhouse close by a deep river, and from the house down to the waterside grew great burdock leaves so high that under the tallest of them a little child could stand upright. The spot was as wild as the center of a thick wood. In this snug retreat sat a duck on her nest, watching for her young brood to hatch; she was beginning to get tired of her task, for the little ones were a long time coming out of their shells, and she seldom had any visitors. The other ducks liked much better to swim about in the river than to climb the slippery banks, and sit under a burdock leaf to have a gossip with her. At length one shell cracked, and then another, and from each egg came a living creature that lifted its head and cried, "Peep, peep." "Quack, quack," said the mother, and then they all quacked as well as they could, and looked about them on every side at the large green leaves. Their mother allowed them to look as much as they liked, because green is good for the eyes. "How large the world is," said the young ducks, when they found how much more room they now had than while they were inside the eggshell. "Do you imagine this is the whole world?" asked the mother. "Wait till you have seen the garden; it stretches far beyond that to the parson's field, but I have never ventured to such a distance. Are you all out?" she continued, rising. "No, I declare, the largest egg lies there still. I wonder how long this is to last, I am quite tired of it," and she seated herself again on the nest.

"Well, how are you getting on?" asked an old duck, who paid her a visit.

"One egg has not hatched yet," said the duck, "it will not break. But just look at all the others, are they not the prettiest little ducklings you ever saw? They are the image of their father, who is so unkind, he never comes to see."

"Let me see the egg that will not break," said the duck. "I have no doubt it is a turkey's egg. I was persuaded to hatch some once, and after all my care and trouble with the young ones, they were afraid of the water. I quacked and clucked, but all to no purpose. I could not get them to venture in. Let me look at the egg. Yes, that is a turkey's egg; take my advice, leave it where it is and teach the other children to swim."

"I think I will sit on it a little while longer," said the duck, "as I have sat so long already, a few days will be nothing."

"Please yourself," said the old duck, and she went away.

At last the large egg broke, and a young one crept forth crying, "Peep, peep." It was very large and ugly. The duck stared at it and exclaimed, "It is very large and not at all like the others. I wonder if it really is a turkey. We shall soon find it out, however, when we go to the water. It must go in, if I have to push it myself."

On the next day the weather was delightful, and the sun shone brightly on the green burdock leaves, so the mother duck took her young brood down to the water and jumped in with a splash. "Quack, quack," cried she, and one after another the little ducklings jumped in. The water closed over their heads, but they came up again in an instant and swam about quite prettily with their legs paddling under them as easily as possible, and the ugly duckling was also in the water swimming with them.

"Oh," said the mother, "that is not a turkey; how well he uses his legs, and how upright he holds himself! He is my own child, and he is not so very ugly after all if you look at him properly. Quack, quack! Come with me now, I will take you into grand society, and introduce you to the farmyard, but you must keep close to me or you may be trodden upon; and, above all, beware of the cat."

When they reached the farmyard, there was a great disturbance; two families were fighting for an eel's head, which, after all, was carried off by the cat. "See, children, that is the way of the world," said the mother duck, whetting her beak, for she would have liked the eel's head herself. "Come, now, use your legs, and let me see how well you can behave. You must bow your heads prettily to that old duck yonder; she is the highest born of them all, and has elite blood; therefore, she is well off. Don't you see she has a red flag tied to her leg, which is something very grand, and a great honor for a duck; it shows that everyone is anxious not to lose her, as she can be recognized both by man and beast. Come, now, don't turn your toes, a well-bred duckling spreads his feet wide apart, just like his father and mother, in this way; now bend your neck, and say 'quack.'"

The ducklings did as they were bid, but the other duck stared, and said, "Look, here comes another brood, as if there were not enough of us already! And what an odd-looking object one of them is; we don't want him here," and then one flew out and bit him in the neck.

"Let him alone," said the mother, "he is not doing any harm."

"Yes, but he is so big and ugly," said the spiteful duck, "and therefore he must be turned out."

"The others are very pretty children," said the old duck with the rag on her leg, "all but that one; I wish his mother could improve him a little."

"That is impossible, Your Grace," replied the mother. "He is not pretty; but he has a very good disposition, and swims as well or even better than the others. I think he will grow up pretty, and perhaps be smaller; he has remained too long in the egg, and therefore his figure is not properly formed," and then she stroked his neck and smoothed the feathers, saying, "It is a drake, and therefore not of so much consequence. I think he will grow up strong and able to take care of himself."

"The other ducklings are graceful enough," said the old duck. "Now make yourself at home, and if you can find an eel's head, you can bring it to me."

And so they made themselves comfortable; but the poor duckling, who had crept out of his shell last of all, and looked so ugly, was bitten and pushed and made fun of, not only by the ducks, but by all the birds. "He is too big," they all said, and the turkey, who had been born into the world with spurs, and fancied himself really an emperor, puffed himself out like a vessel in full sail and flew at the duckling, and became quite red in the head with passion, so that the poor little thing did not know where to go, and was quite miserable because he was so ugly and laughed at by the whole farmyard. So it went on from day to day till it got worse and worse. The poor duckling was driven about by everyone; even his brothers and sisters were unkind to him, and would say, "Ah, you ugly creature, I wish the cat would get you," and his mother said she wished he had never been born. The ducks pecked him, the chickens beat him, and the girl who fed the birds kicked him with her feet. So at last he ran away, frightening the little birds in the hedge as he flew over the palings.

"They are afraid of me because I am ugly," he said. So

he closed his eyes and flew still farther, until he came out on a large moor inhabited by wild ducks. Here he remained the whole night, feeling very tired and sorrowful.

In the morning, when the wild ducks rose in the air, they stared at their new comrade. "What sort of a duck are you?" they all said, coming around him.

He bowed to them, and was as polite as he could be, but he did not reply to their question. "You are exceedingly ugly," said the wild ducks, "but that will not matter if you do not want to marry one of our family."

Poor thing! He had no thoughts of marriage; all he wanted was permission to lie among the rushes, and drink some of the water on the moor. After he had been on the moor two days, there came two wild geese, or rather goslings, for they had not been out of the egg long, and were very saucy. "Listen, friend," said one of them to the duckling, "you are so ugly, that we like you very well.

Will you go with us and become a bird of passage? Not far from here is another moor, in which there are some pretty wild geese, all unmarried. It is a chance for you to get a wife; you may be lucky, ugly as you are."

Pop, pop, sounded in the air, and the two wild geese fell dead among the rushes, and the water was tinged with blood. *Pop, pop*, echoed far and wide in the distance, and whole flocks of wild geese rose up from the rushes. The sound continued from every direction, for the sportsmen surrounded the moor, and some were even seated on branches of trees, overlooking the rushes. The blue smoke from the guns rose like clouds over the dark trees, and as it floated away across the water, a number of sporting dogs bounded in among the rushes, which bent beneath them wherever they went. How they terrified the poor duckling! He turned away his head to hide it under his wing, and at the same moment a large terrible dog passed quite near him. His jaws were open, his tongue hung from his mouth, and his eyes glared fearfully. He thrust his nose close to the duckling, showing his sharp teeth, and then, *splash*, *splash*, he went into the water without touching him. "Oh," sighed the duckling, "how thankful I am for being so ugly; even a dog will not bite me." And so he lay quite still, while the shot rattled through the rushes, and gun after gun was fired over him. It was late in the day before all became quiet, but even then the poor young thing did not dare to move. He waited quietly for several hours, and then, after looking carefully around him, hastened away from the moor as fast as he could. He ran over field and meadow till a storm arose, and he could hardly struggle against it. Toward evening, he reached a poor little cottage that seemed ready to fall, and only remained standing because it could not decide on which side to fall first. The storm continued so violent that the duckling could go no farther; he sat down by the cottage, and then he noticed that the door was not quite closed in consequence of one of the hinges having given way. There was therefore a narrow opening near the bottom large enough for him to slip through, which he did very quietly, and got a shelter for the night. A woman, a tomcat, and a hen lived in this cottage. The cat, whom the mistress called, "My little son," was a great favorite. He could raise his back and purr and could even throw out sparks from his fur if it was stroked the wrong way. The hen had very short legs, so she was called "Chickie short legs." She laid good eggs, and her mistress loved her as if she had been her own child. In the morning, the strange visitor was discovered, and the cat began to purr and the hen to cluck.

"What is that noise about?" said the old woman, looking around the room, but her sight was not very good; therefore, when she saw the duckling she thought it must be a fat duck that had strayed from home. "Oh, what a prize!" she exclaimed. "I hope it is not a drake, for then I shall have some duck's eggs. I must wait and see." So the duckling was allowed to remain on trial for three weeks, but there were no eggs. Now the cat was the master of the house, and the hen was mistress, and they always said, "We and the world," for they believed themselves to be half the world, and the better half, too. The duckling thought that others might hold a different opinion on the subject, but the hen would not listen to such doubts. "Can you lay eggs?" she asked.

"No."

"Then have the goodness to hold your tongue." "Can you raise your back, or purr, or throw out sparks?" said the cat.

"No."

"Then you have no right to express an opinion when sensible people are speaking." So the duckling sat in a corner, feeling very low spirited, till the sunshine and the fresh air came into the room through the open door, and then he began to feel such a great longing for a swim on the water that he could not help telling the hen.

"What an absurd idea," said the hen. "You have nothing else to do, therefore you have foolish fancies. If you could purr or lay eggs, they would pass away."

"But it is so delightful to swim about on the water," said the duckling, "and so refreshing to feel it close over your head while you dive down to the bottom."

"Delightful, indeed!" said the hen. "Why, you must be crazy! Ask the cat, he is the cleverest animal I know; ask him how he would like to swim about on the water, or to dive under it, for I will not speak of my own opinion; ask our mistress, the old woman—there is no one in the world more clever than she is. Do you think she would like to swim, or to let the water close over her head?"

"You don't understand me," said the duckling.

"We don't understand you? Who can understand you, I wonder? Do you consider yourself more clever than the cat, or the old woman? I will say nothing of myself. Don't imagine such nonsense, child, and thank your good fortune that you have been received here. Are you not in a warm room and in society from which you may learn something. But you are a chatterer, and your company is not very agreeable. Believe me, I speak only for your own good. I may tell you unpleasant truths, but that is a proof of my friendship. I advise you, therefore, to lay eggs and learn to purr as quickly as possible."

"I believe I must go out into the world again," said the duckling.

"Yes, do," said the hen. So the duckling left the cottage and soon found water on which it could swim and dive, but was avoided by all other animals because of its ugly appearance. Autumn came, and the leaves in the forest turned to orange and gold. Then, as winter approached, the wind caught them as they fell and whirled in the cold air. The clouds, heavy with hail and snowflakes, hung low in the sky, and the raven stood on the ferns crying, "Croak, croak." It made one shiver with cold to look at him. All this was very sad for the poor little duckling. One evening, just as the sun set amid radiant clouds, there came a large flock of beautiful birds out of the bushes. The duckling had never seen any like them before. They were swans, and they curved their graceful necks, while their soft plumage shown with dazzling whiteness. They uttered a singular cry as they spread their glorious wings and flew away from those cold regions to warmer countries across the sea. As they mounted higher and higher in the air, the ugly little duckling felt quite a strange sensation as he watched them. He whirled himself in the water like a wheel, stretched out his neck toward them, and uttered a cry so strange that it frightened himself. Could he ever forget those beautiful, happy birds; and when at last they were out of his sight, he dived under the water and rose again almost beside himself with excitement. He knew not the names of these birds, nor where they had flown, but he felt toward them as he had never felt for any other bird in the world. He was not envious of these beautiful creatures, but wished to be as lovely as they. Poor ugly creature, how gladly he would have lived even with the ducks had they only given him encouragement. The winter grew colder and colder; he was obliged to swim about on the water to keep it from freezing, but every night the space on which he swam became smaller and smaller. At length it froze so hard that the ice in the water crackled as he moved, and the duckling had to paddle with his legs as well as he could to keep the space from closing up. He became exhausted at last, and lay still and helpless, frozen fast in the ice.

Early in the morning, a peasant, who was passing by, saw what had happened. He broke the ice in pieces with his wooden shoe and carried the duckling home to his wife. The warmth revived the poor little creature; but when the children wanted to play with him, the duckling thought they would do him some harm; so he started up in terror, fluttered into the milk pan, and splashed the milk about the room. Then the woman clapped her hands, which frightened him still more. He flew first into the butter cask, then into the meal tub, and out again. What a condition he was in! The woman screamed, and struck at him with the tongs; the children laughed and screamed and tumbled over each other in their efforts to catch him, but luckily he escaped. The door stood open; the poor creature could just manage to slip out among the bushes and lie down quite exhausted in the newly fallen snow.

It would be very sad, were I to relate all the misery and privations which the poor little duckling endured during the hard winter; but when it had passed, he found himself lying one morning in a moor, among the rushes. He felt the warm sun shining, and heard the lark singing, and saw that all around was beautiful spring. Then the young bird felt that his wings were strong as he flapped them against his sides and rose high into the air. They bore him onward, until he found himself in a large garden, before he well knew how it had happened. The apple trees were in full blossom, and the fragrant elders bent their long green branches down to the stream which wound around a smooth lawn. Everything looked beautiful in the freshness of early spring. From a thicket close by came three beautiful white swans, rustling their feathers and swimming lightly over the smooth water. The duckling remembered the lovely birds, and felt more strangely unhappy than ever.

"I will fly to those royal birds," he exclaimed, "and

they will kill me, because I am so ugly and dare to approach them; but it does not matter: Better be killed by them than pecked by the ducks, beaten by the hens, pushed about by the maiden who feeds the poultry, or starved with hunger in the winter."

Then he flew to the water and swam toward the beautiful swans. The moment they espied the stranger, they rushed to meet him with outstretched wings.

"Kill me," said the poor bird, and he bent his head down to the surface of the water and awaited death.

But what did he see in the clear stream below? His own image; no longer a dark, gray bird, ugly and disagreeable to look at, but a graceful and beautiful swan. To be born in a duck's nest, in a farmyard, is of no consequence to a bird if it is hatched from a swan's egg. He now felt glad at having suffered sorrow and trouble, because it enabled him to enjoy so much better all the pleasure and happiness around him; for the great swans swam around the newcomer and stroked his neck with their beaks as a welcome.

Into the garden presently came some little children, and threw bread and cake into the water.

"See," cried the youngest. "There is a new one," and the rest were delighted and ran to their father and mother, dancing and clapping their hands and shouting joyously. "There is another swan come; a new one has arrived."

Then they threw more bread and cake into the water, and said, "The new one is the most beautiful of all; he is so young and pretty." And the old swans bowed their heads before him.

Then he felt quite ashamed and hid his head under his wing, for he did not know what to do. He was so happy, and yet not at all proud. He had been persecuted and despised for his ugliness, and now he heard them say he was the most beautiful of all the birds. Even the elder tree bent down its bows into the water before him, and the sun shone warm and bright. Then he rustled his feathers, curved his slender neck, and cried joyfully from the depths of his heart, "I never dreamed of such happiness as this, while I was an ugly duckling."